Intently, Dante stared at her, and could feel the powerful beat of his heart. 'Is there something you need to tell me?'

Justina nodded as a wave of emotion threatened to overwhelm her, but she held it back. Don't act coy, or ashamed or intimidated, she urged herself. Just deal with the facts.

'Is that a roundabout way of asking whether you're the father?'

'Am I?'

For a moment she hesitated, tempted to tell him that, no, he wasn't. But then she thought of the child she carried. The baby who was currently kicking beneath her fluttering heart as if it was trying out for a foetal football team. Could she wilfully deny her child the knowledge of its father just because that father didn't love *her*?

'Yes,' she breathed—and then she said it again, so that there could be no going back. 'Yes, you are the father, Dante.'

D0610149

Sharon Kendrick started story-telling at the age of eleven, and has never really stopped. She likes to write fast-paced, feel-good romances with heroes who are so sexy they'll make your toes curl!

Born in west London, she now lives in the beautiful city of Winchester—where she can see the cathedral from her window (but only if she stands on tiptoe). She has two children, Celia and Patrick, and her passions include music, books, cooking and eating—and drifting off into wonderful daydreams while she works out new plots!

Recent titles by the same author:

BACK IN THE HEADLINES
  (Scandal in the Spotlight)
A TAINTED BEAUTY
THE SHEIKH'S HEIR
  (The Santina Crown)
PLAYING THE GREEK'S GAME

**Did you know these are also available as eBooks?
Visit www.millsandboon.co.uk**

A SCANDAL,
A SECRET, A BABY

BY
SHARON KENDRICK

All the characters in this book have no existence outside the imagination of the author, and have no relation whatsoever to anyone bearing the same name or names. They are not even distantly inspired by any individual known or unknown to the author, and all the incidents are pure invention.

All Rights Reserved including the right of reproduction in whole or in part in any form. This edition is published by arrangement with Harlequin Enterprises II BV/S.à.r.l. The text of this publication or any part thereof may not be reproduced or transmitted in any form or by any means, electronic or mechanical, including photocopying, recording, storage in an information retrieval system, or otherwise, without the written permission of the publisher.

This book is sold subject to the condition that it shall not, by way of trade or otherwise, be lent, resold, hired out or otherwise circulated without the prior consent of the publisher in any form of binding or cover other than that in which it is published and without a similar condition including this condition being imposed on the subsequent purchaser.

® and TM are trademarks owned and used by the trademark owner and/or its licensee. Trademarks marked with ® are registered with the United Kingdom Patent Office and/or the Office for Harmonisation in the Internal Market and in other countries.

First published in Great Britain 2013
by Mills & Boon, an imprint of Harlequin (UK) Limited.
Harlequin (UK) Limited, Eton House, 18-24 Paradise Road,
Richmond, Surrey TW9 1SR

© Sharon Kendrick 2013

ISBN: 978 0 263 89987 0

Harlequin (UK) policy is to use papers that are natural, renewable and recyclable products and made from wood grown in sustainable forests. The logging and manufacturing process conform to the legal environmental regulations of the country of origin.

Printed and bound in Spain
by Blackprint CPI, Barcelona

A SCANDAL,
A SECRET, A BABY

To Ruth Nehrebecka,
who is a great inspiration
(as well as being enviably blonde and effortlessly stylish!)

CHAPTER ONE

DANTE D'AREZZO KNEW the exact moment his ex-fiancée walked into the cathedral. He heard the silence which fell and the whisper which followed.

'Look, there's Justina Perry.'

And the murmured response. 'Oh, *wow*!'

Dante could feel the punch of his heart as people turned their heads to look at her, to see if she'd changed. They wanted to know if she had any new lines on her face—or whether those lines had been ironed out by surgery. They wanted to know if she was heavier. Or lighter. They wanted to know every damned thing about her, because once she had been famous and fame made people think they owned you.

Dante knew that. He knew that only too damned well. Hadn't he watched from the sidelines long enough to learn about the darker aspects of fame? The way it corrupted and corroded and spread into normal life like some sort of toxic acid?

His powerful body tight with tension, he watched her sinuous progress down the wide aisle of Norwich

Cathedral, where the wedding of her ex-bandmate was shortly to take place. Her dark hair had been coiled into an elaborate confection at the back of her head and she was wearing an oriental-looking gown of pale satin, lavishly embroidered with dragons and flowers. At first glance the dress seemed disappointingly demure—until she moved forward on a pair of towering heels and a thigh-high split revealed the tantalising flash of one long, bare leg.

An unwanted wave of desire swept over him, quickly followed by a powerful surge of anger. So she still liked to show herself off like some kind of cheap *puttana*, did she? Did she still enjoy the sensation of other men watching her and wanting her—fantasising about that sinner's body coupled with the soulful face of a dark angel?

But his anger was not enough to diminish the exquisite ache in his body, and he watched as she took her place in one of the front rows, turning to smile at the person next to her as she sank down onto the pew. The embroidered satin stretched over her delicious bottom and all Dante could think about was how long it had been. Five long years since he'd seen her. More than enough time for him to have become immune to her feline appeal. So why was his heart thundering as he watched her staring up at the altar? Why was the hardening at his groin so pronounced that he was having to cover it up with his hymn sheet?

He tried to think about something else as the marriage service began—but it wasn't easy. Not when this wedding seemed even longer than weddings usually were—probably because the groom just happened to be a duke. Dante always played the part expected of him, and usually he would have been an exemplary and attentive guest. But today, his attention was focussed elsewhere and all the way through the service his thoughts kept straying back to Justina.

Justina writhing beneath him on a snow-white bed.

Justina with her ebony hair and magnolia skin and those amazing amber eyes.

He remembered the sweet tightness of her body. Those tiny little nipples which had been made to fit so perfectly inside a man's mouth. Briefly he shook his head, for those thoughts disturbed him. He wanted to forget that for the first and only time in his life he'd made a mistake. His broken engagement was the only failure in a life which had been charted with resounding success. He was a proud man of noble Tuscan heritage. His ancestors had been scholars, soldiers and diplomats—an aristocratic line which had always been land-rich but cash-poor. But then Dante had become head of the family's business interests and had taken them soaring into the stratosphere.

These days the D'Arezzo family owned property over most of the globe, in addition to their vast vineyards in the beautiful countryside outside Florence. Dante had everything a man could possibly want, and yet inside his heart was empty.

There were bells ringing now—a triumphant peal of them heralding the end of the ceremony. And then came the somewhat unbelievable sight of Roxy Carmichael—all misty in white silk and pearls—clinging on to the arm of her new husband, the Duke. Dante shook his head in slight disbelief. Who would ever have thought it? The last time he'd seen Roxy she had been dancing around on a giant stage wearing little more than a sequinned pelmet which had been masquerading as a skirt.

That was what they'd all used to wear when she, Justina and Lexi had made up the Lollipops—the biggest girl-band on the planet. When for a while he had been little more than a member of their extensive posse.

The congregation had begun to file out behind the bride and groom and Dante found himself watching. Wanting to see Justina's reaction when she saw him sitting there. Did she ever regret the choices she'd made? The ones which had led to his rejection of her? Did she ever lie in bed thinking and fretting about what could have been hers?

Last night he had given in to a temptation he'd long resisted, and a quick search on his computer had told him that Justina remained unmarried, with no children—something which had given him pause for thought. She must be nearly thirty now, he realised. Wasn't she worried that these days women were advised to have children sooner, rather than later? A cruel smile curved the edges of his lips. No, of course she wasn't.

What appeal would a child have to someone like her? Her career was everything to her. *Everything.*

His gaze flicked over her pale skin as she came towards him and for one suspended moment he saw her footsteps falter when their gazes met and locked. He looked into her amber eyes, which looked golden against the sudden snowy pallor of her skin. Saw them widen in disbelief and then saw a flash of something in their depths which he couldn't have defined even if he could be bothered to try. What Justina Perry thought or felt was of no interest to him. Not any more. But he wouldn't have been human if he hadn't enjoyed the sudden swallowing movement he observed rippling down over that swanlike neck of hers.

She was right beside him now. Close enough for him to catch a drift of her perfume, which made him think of jasmine and honey. And then she was gone, and he was aware of a pretty blonde in the row in front of him, who was turning round to give him a very bright smile indeed.

But the smile Dante returned was perfunctory. He hadn't come here today to find a woman. Though he hadn't really stopped to ask himself why he'd accepted an invitation he'd never been expecting to receive. Was it to lay a ghost to rest? To convince himself that he now felt nothing for the only woman who had ever managed to penetrate the stony exterior of his hard Tuscan heart?

He walked out into the crisp brightness of the day, where he could smell the powerful scent of the flowers which were arching around the vast doors of the cathedral. He looked across the courtyard to where Justina stood, surrounded by people clamouring for her attention—but she wasn't listening to them. Her attention was fixed on the door, as if she'd been waiting for him to appear, and as her eyes found their target in him he felt the thrill of something he could never have described—not even in his native tongue.

He began to walk towards her, only vaguely aware of the women who turned to watch his progress—women watching him was something which had happened throughout his charmed life. He saw Justina's teeth dig into the pink cushion of her bottom lip, and as he remembered just what those beautiful lips were capable of a stab of lust threatened to overwhelm him.

He had reached her now, and the people surrounding her grew quiet as faces were turned towards him in open curiosity. He guessed that the novelty of his dark Italian looks was enough to arouse interest in this most English of settings. And maybe his face looked as forbidding as he intended it to look, because they quickly moved away, so that the two of them were left alone.

'Well, well, well,' he said. 'Look who's here.'

Justina stared up at him, her heart pounding in a way it hadn't done in a long, long time. She could feel her senses firing into life as if someone had just set light to them. She could feel the prickle of her breasts and the instant pooling of liquid heat and she was praying that the cheating bastard wouldn't guess. She didn't *want* to desire him. She wanted to present a cool and unruffled exterior. But it wasn't easy. Not when his face was just inches away from hers—a face more beautiful and yet more elementally savage than any other she'd ever seen. His dark eyes were boring into her and his powerful body was imprinting itself into her consciousness. She felt weak. As if someone had just drained away all her blood and replaced it with water.

Well, you're stronger than that, she told herself. *You aren't going to show any sign of weakness. Because this is Dante D'Arezzo. The man who confuses love with control. Who dumped you because you wouldn't behave like his own personal puppet. Who cold-bloodedly took another woman to his bed and...and....*

She saw a bed with rumpled sheets. A mass of ruffled blond hair and a high, pert bottom. And Dante, his eyes closed, a smile of ecstasy on his cheating lips as the naked woman administered to his every need.

The vivid images of his betrayal were like jagged pieces of glass at the edges of her mind and Justina only just managed to blunt them—just as she'd spent the last five years blunting them. She mustn't think of that. She couldn't afford to. She had to focus on what was important—and the only thing she could think of right then was making him go away and leave her alone.

She kept her expression unwelcoming, her voice a cool drawl. 'Thanks for ruining what could have been a perfectly good day,' she said. 'Who invited you?'

Dante hadn't been expecting such *open* hostility,

and for some reason that he wasn't quite able to work out this pleased him. Was it because the prospect of a fight with her was almost as tantalising as the thought of spreading her over the bonnet of that nearby car and riding her until he came?

He took a stealthy step closer. 'Who do you think invited me? The bride, of course. Or did you imagine that I gatecrashed?'

Justina couldn't suppress a faint shiver as his powerful form cast a shadow over her like a dark omen. As if Dante had ever had to gatecrash anything in his life!

'Really?' she questioned, wishing that she could stop reacting to him like this.

She felt as if her body had suddenly started thawing after spending years in some arctic waste. As if she would die if she didn't touch him again, or feel those hard lips pressing down on hers. She found herself remembering the way he'd used to put his head between her legs and lick her there, and she shivered with shameful longing. How did he *do* that? How could he still make her want him when she hated him so much?

'I didn't even think you were still in touch with Roxy.'

'I wasn't. We lost contact a long while ago—about the time when you and I split.' His dark eyes mocked her. 'But presumably she was feeling generously disposed towards the world when she found herself a duke to marry, and so she decided to track me down.'

Justina knew exactly why Roxy had done it. A man

like Dante would be a luminary on any guest list; his
grandness and stature would be a boost to any hostess's
street-cred. And, of course, his outstanding good looks
would guarantee that all the single female guests would
be purring with contentment. But why the hell hadn't
Roxy bothered to warn her about it beforehand? Had
her ex-bandmate guessed that she wouldn't have come
within a hundred miles of the church if she'd known *he*
was going to be here?

Yet surely she should be immune to him by now?
She hadn't seen him for nearly five years. She was older
and supposedly a whole lot wiser—wise enough for his
undeniable sex appeal to leave her cold. *So why wasn't
that happening?* Why were her breasts tingling as his
arrogant gaze skated over her, that molten aching at her
thighs making her feel embarrassingly self-conscious?

With a feigned composure she stared at him—praying for an objectivity she'd never been able to apply to
this Tuscan aristocrat. He was wearing a suit, like every
other man there—apart from the few guests in uniform
—but something about the *way* he wore it instantly
marked him out as someone special. The exquisite cut
of the charcoal cloth hugged his powerful frame, em-
phasising the narrow jut of his hips and the definition
of his long legs. Yet despite his highly sophisticated
exterior, with Dante D'Arezzo all you were aware of
was the primitive man beneath. He was the sort of man
who saw what he wanted and went out and took it. Who

made women cry with pleasure. And with pain, she reminded herself. With terrible and lasting pain.

'Maybe Roxy was short on numbers and that was the reason for your out-of-the-blue invitation,' she said as she glanced up at the cathedral with a flippant shrug. 'It's a pretty big church to fill. And I expect a token Tuscan aristocrat is on every bride's wish list.'

He smiled, as if her insult meant nothing to him—as if he guessed that it was all for show. 'It's been a long time, Justina,' he said softly.

'Five years.' Her smile was fixed. 'Time flies when you're having fun—something which was certainly in short supply when I was engaged to you.'

But he didn't appear to be listening. His gaze was drifting slowly over her body as if he still had the right to look at her that way. As if she was his possession and he owned her.

'You've lost weight,' he said.

She felt her heart miss a beat, unsure if it was caused by disappointment or anger—because wasn't that just typical of Dante? For him to take something she felt proud of and make it sound like something bad. She'd worked very hard for this body. Dragged herself out of bed on the most inhospitable of mornings to pound the pavements, come rain or shine. When she was travelling, she was a frequent visitor to hotel gyms—padding the anonymous carpeted corridors at unsociable hours while she listened to music from her earphones. And hadn't her strict regime rescued her from the essential loneliness of those solitary hotel stays?

She never ate carbs after 5:00 p.m., and she rarely drank alcohol. She was disciplined about her lifestyle because it was harder to stay fit the older you got. And physical fitness helped her to cope. It kept her fresh and alert in an industry where youth was everything—an industry which she'd seen claim the lives of those who couldn't cope with its impossibly high demands. And she had sacrificed too much for her to career to do anything to ever jeopardise it.

'Well, isn't that fortunate? Since losing weight was what I was aiming for,' she responded, her gaze flicking over his charcoal-grey suit, which was doing nothing to disguise the hard musculature beneath. 'You might try working out a little yourself some time, Dante. Try for the leaner look—it's very fashionable, you know.'

'I don't think so. I get all the exercise I need without the narcissistic need to spend hours down at the gym.' He leaned forward by a fraction, noting the automatic dilatation of her eyes as he did so, and suddenly he wanted her. Wanted her so badly that he could have pulled her into his arms and crushed those cushioned lips beneath the hungry clamour of his own. His eyes glinted. 'My body is hard in all the places it needs to be hard.'

Justina felt her face grow hot, as unsettled by his sudden closeness as by the unashamedly sexual boast, and she took a step back. 'You're disgusting.'

'You think so? You used to like my particular brand of disgusting, as I recall.'

'That was a long time ago. Fortunately I've grown up since then. My tastes have matured and I'm no longer attracted to the Neanderthal type.'

'Then you really *must* have changed. I've never known a woman who was so turned on by a man being masterful in bed.'

His silky taunt whispered towards her and brought back memories Justina thought she'd buried for ever. Memories of Dante kissing her. Dante pushing his hardness deep into her warm, wet heat. *Dante doing that to another woman.* She wanted to scream. To lash out at him and ask why he'd done it—*why?* But she would not give in to the pointlessness of resurrecting the past. The past was over. Her life was now and her future didn't involve him.

And she needed to get away from him.

Directing her gaze to an imaginary spot behind his head, she forced her mouth into a smile of recognition, as if she'd just seen someone she knew, so that by the time she allowed herself to look into those dark eyes again she had composed herself enough to adopt a convincing air of indifference.

'You really mustn't let me monopolise you any longer, Dante. I'm sure there are lots of people who are longing to speak to you. In fact there's a young lady over there who seems eager to catch your eye. I'm sure you'll still be quick enough off the mark to have her in your bed before the day is out.'

And then she began to walk away, half afraid that he might try to stop her. But he did no such thing. She saw the brief narrowing of his eyes as she turned on her towering heels and walked across the cathedral square, and she was aware of the burn of his gaze as she allowed herself to be swallowed up in a group of guests. Her hands were trembling and her heart was racing and for a moment she contemplated leaving the wedding right then. Nothing was stopping her. She could hurry back to the hotel she'd booked into, pack up her stuff and head back to London. She could run away from her ex-fiancé and all the painful memories that seeing him again evoked.

But Justina knew she couldn't do that. She and Roxy had only recently been reunited, and she couldn't let her old friend down on such an important day. Averting her face from a paparazzi camera which seemed to have sprung from out of nowhere, she gave a ragged sigh. She was just going to have to behave like a grown-up and deal with it. She would go to the wedding reception and avoid Dante. How hard could it be? She was good at avoiding people—and she doubted that he'd be on his own for long.

She made her way towards the line of red double-decker buses which had been hired to take all the guests to the reception and found a seat, smiling politely at the man who immediately slid in next to her and started to introduce himself. But it was difficult to concentrate on what he was saying, even though he was doing his level best to flirt and was wearing a whole row of bright medals on his military uniform. He was probably some kind of dashing war hero, she thought gloomily, as well as being handsome in that blond and square-jawed sort of way.

So why could she never be attracted to someone like him—the sort of man she knew she *should* be attracted to? The dependable type who might easily adore her if only she'd give them half a chance. Wasn't it a mark of her own emotional failure that nobody had ever come close to making her feel the way that Dante had done? And wasn't that the main reason why she was still single as thirty loomed on the horizon—with no stable relationship and the chances of having a baby receding with every year that passed?

She remembered the magazine interview she'd given only last week, when the persistent journalist had managed to make her confront that uncomfortable fact. That if she waited too long she might never have a baby of her own. Feeling cornered, Justina had said that of *course* she wanted a baby. And then had added jokily that first she would need to find someone to be her baby's father!

The double-decker bus lumbered through the narrow Norfolk lanes before turning in to the grand gates which led to the Duke's estate. A long, gravelled drive swept up to the groom's ancestral home and as the bus halted outside, Justina felt the breath catch in her throat as she glanced up at the perfectly proportioned golden building which Roxy had told her so much about.

Surrounded by green parkland, Valeo Hall was guarded by two snarling bronze lions which stood on top of two plinths. The pillars lining the steps up to the massive oak door were garlanded with the same fragrant white flowers which had decorated the cathedral, and Justina breathed in their sweet scent as she stepped down onto the forecourt. Lucky Roxy, she found herself thinking. A new husband and a new life. A whole new future just sitting waiting for them. Surely she wouldn't have been human if she hadn't felt a moment of wistful envy at that moment?

Standing in line, waiting to congratulate the newlyweds, she gave the handsome Duke a quick hug and seconds later was enveloped in a cloud of tulle and white lace as his bride stepped forward to embrace her tightly.

'Oh, Jus.' Roxy beamed. 'I'm so glad you could come! Did you enjoy the service?'

'It was gorgeous. *You* look gorgeous—the loveliest bride I've ever seen. But you didn't tell me that Dante was going to be here,' Justina whispered.

'Should I have done?' Roxy smiled in a conspiratorial way which made her look about nineteen again. 'I know you aren't together now, but I thought I'd invite him anyway—because for a while, Dante was a big part of my life. You don't mind, do you?'

Justina gave a wry smile. What could she say? That seeing him again had been like revisiting an unbearably dark and painful place? She looked at Roxy's luminous face and reminded herself that this was about more than her own hurt pride and wounded heart. This was *Roxy's* day—and surely she could suffer seeing Dante one more time for her sake?

'Of course I don't mind,' she said cheerfully. 'Always good to get a blast from the past.'

Touching her fingertips to her diamond tiara as if checking it was still there, Roxy frowned. 'So there's nothing going on between you any more?'

'You're kidding?' Justina's denial was vehement and heartfelt. 'Dante and I are history.'

She moved aside to make way for the next guest and took a glass of champagne from a passing waitress. Raising the glass to her lips, she drank more quickly than normal—but the quick hit of fizzy wine made rebellion begin to simmer inside her as she walked towards the reception. Why *should* she allow herself to be intimidated by Dante D'Arezzo when she was strong enough to stand up to him? She was an independent woman, wasn't she? Not some little mouse. If she ran into him at the reception—and that was a big *if*, since she intended to stay as far away from him as possible— then she would stonewall him, just as she'd managed to do outside the church today.

She looked around. Guests were beginning to file into the vast banqueting hall which had been laid with individual tables. The golden and white room was hung with chandeliers, blazing splintering light over the heirloom crystal and silver. Here there were more pillars, all woven with ivy and spring flowers, and Justina had the sense of having walked into an enchanted glade where anything could happen.

She found her name on the seating plan, pleased to discover that she was sandwiched between a brigadier-general—which meant that he would probably be about eighty—and a Lord Aston, who she'd never heard of. But her main source of pleasure came from the fact that she was nowhere near Dante. At least Roxy had been diplomatic enough to seat them on opposite sides of the room.

She made her way across the shiny floor of the banqueting hall towards her table, but her extra-high heels and her cheongsam dress meant that all her attention was focussed on making the journey without mishap. She wasn't really paying attention to the other guests who were taking their places, and it wasn't until an olive hand reached over to pull out her chair that some internal warning system began to sound.

Justina froze with a terrible sense of inevitability as she looked down into the brilliant dark gaze of the man she had once thought would be her husband.

CHAPTER TWO

HER HEART RACING with fury and an unwanted kind of excitement, Justina stared into Dante's dark face—wishing she could wipe that supercilious smile from his lips. 'What the hell are *you* doing here?' she said viciously, and an emerald-decked redhead sitting opposite jerked up her head in surprise.

'Do keep your voice down, Justina,' he said. 'This is an aristocratic wedding where name-calling will almost certainly not be tolerated.'

Justina could have shaken him. Or punched against that solid wall of a chest. Or…*something*. Something which involved stamping her foot like a child and demanding that he be removed from her proximity as quickly as possible. As it was, she could do little except sit down in the chair which he was now pulling out for her. Because he was right. This was the wedding of one of her oldest friends and she could hardly cause a scene by demanding that she be moved to a different seat, could she?

He had risen to his feet and was helping her into her

chair, his fingers briefly brushing over her shoulders before he slid into the vacant chair beside her.

She turned to look at him, careful to keep her voice low even though she could feel her nerve ends screaming in response to that unexpected touch of his hands. 'I'm surprised you even know the meaning of the word "tolerate",' she said. 'How did you manage to get here before me when I was on the first bus?'

'I drove.'

Justina nodded. He'd driven. Of course he had. Could she really imagine him obediently trooping onto the transport provided like everybody else? He was the ultimate control freak, and whatever happened it always had to be on *his* terms.

She sucked in a deep breath. 'What I don't understand is why you happen to be sitting *here*?'

'For exactly the same reason as you, I imagine. Waiting for the wedding breakfast to begin, and with it the opportunity to toast the bride and groom and wish them many happy years of wedded bliss.'

'Please don't wilfully misunderstand me, Dante. That's not what I meant and you know it.' Reluctantly Justina's eyes focussed on the hard planes of his face, which were softened only by the sensual curves of his lips. She saw the faint shadow at his jaw which always appeared, no matter how often he shaved.

Why did he have to be so damned *sexy*? she thought. And why was her traitorous body reacting so hungrily to him as she breathed in his warm and earthy scent?

'I looked at the table plan and your name was no-where near mine. I was just celebrating my good fortune at such a sympathetic placement and now I find you next to me. So how did that happen, Dante?'

'Simple. I changed the names,' he said unrepentantly.

Justina glared at him. How could she have forgotten his high-handedness? That way he had of just blazing in and taking whatever it was he wanted as if the world was just one giant boardroom? 'You can't turn up at a posh society wedding and start rearranging the seating!'

'I just did.' He sat back in his seat and glittered her a lazy smile. 'And since no one else has a problem with it I suggest you go with the flow and enjoy yourself.'

'Enjoy myself? With you beside me? That's a joke, right?' She bent to put her bag on the floor, mainly in an attempt to disguise the sudden tremble of her fingers. 'If I wanted to spend the afternoon in the company of a snake I'd head for the nearest pit.'

Dante saw the mutinous look on her face as she lifted her head again and for a moment he almost smiled. How could he have forgotten her outrageous defiance—the only woman in the world who had not deferred to his wishes? Who had been determined to get her voice heard and insisted that her career was just as important as his.

For a while he had enjoyed their delicious battle of wills, with the subsequent make-up sessions which had been all about red-hot passion. Until he'd been forced to realise that she meant what she said. That her objections had not been some sustained sexual tease and that she had no intention of compromising her lifestyle after their marriage. She was a singer and a performer, she'd told him, and she'd been given opportunities which came along all too rarely. She'd told him she couldn't—no—she *wouldn't* turn them down. She'd also smilingly had the nerve to tell him to stop being such a dinosaur and to respect how important her career was. But behind her smile had been the definite glint of steel, and that had unsettled him. He remembered being furious and then—surprisingly—hurt. Until he'd forced himself to be grateful for his lucky escape. Because her attitude did not bode well for a long-term relationship with someone like him.

His thoughts cleared and he found himself looking into clear amber eyes which were framed so exquisitely by her dark lashes. He waited until their wine had been poured and then let his gaze linger on her bare left hand.

'So. No wedding band. I note that you have not been as fortunate as your bandmate in the matrimonial stakes,' he observed.

Pausing midmouthful of wine, Justina almost choked with indignation. 'The matrimonial *stakes*! It's not some kind of horse race!'

'No?' He shrugged. 'But it *is* a race, all the same. Most women like to be in a permanent relationship by the time they're your age because they are thinking about the inevitable ticking of their biological clock. What are you now, Justina? Thirty-one? Thirty-two?'

'I'm not even thirty!' she gritted out, and it wasn't until she saw the answering gleam in his eyes that she realised she had fallen into some horrible sort of trap.

She'd ended up sounding defensive about her age, just because she was about to leave her twenties behind without a wedding ring on her finger. Dante had managed to do what Dante always did so well—he'd made her feel bad about herself.

So don't let him! She slanted him an adversarial look. 'I think these days you'll find an emerging breed of women who don't need the mark of a man's possession to define themselves.'

'I see your rather aggressively feminist stance hasn't softened with time.'

'Feeling threatened, are you?'

'Believe me, Justina—I'm feeling something a lot more basic than threatened.'

His mocking gaze had flickered to his groin and Justina felt her cheeks grow hot with a mixture of anger and desire. Viciously, she jabbed her fork into an unsuspecting spear of asparagus, though she couldn't quite bring herself to eat it. What was the *matter* with her? He was insulting her, and even if he *did* underpin the insults with a deliberate sensuality why the hell was she responding like this?

She put her fork back down. Perhaps that was what absence did? It hadn't made her heart grow any fonder, but it had certainly awoken a sexual appetite which she had thought gone for ever. And Dante was the last person she wanted to make her feel this way. As if she'd been wandering around, starved of all comfort and pleasure, until he had suddenly reappeared, symbolising everything she'd been missing in one dark and very dangerous package.

'Did you go to all the trouble of rearranging your seat just so that you could spend the entire meal being objectionable?' she questioned.

'Oh, come on, Justina. You know exactly why I did it. Surely you can appreciate that I am a little *curious* about you—especially considering that we were once planning to be man and wife?'

'You mean until you decided that you'd have sex with that…that…' She wanted to spit out the word *tart* or *whore*—but that might give him the erroneous impression that she still cared. Picking up her wine glass, she knocked back a large mouthful. '*Woman*,' she finished acidly.

'Will you stop rewriting history?' he demanded. 'You know damned well that we'd already broken up by then.'

She opened her mouth to object, and then shut it again—because what was the point? He arrogantly refused to see that he'd done anything wrong and nothing she said was going to change his mind. *So let it go. Stop reacting to him, because that's what he wants you to do.*

Yet it felt like hell to be this close to him. Trying like mad to pretend that she felt nothing when inside her heart was beating so loudly she was surprised that someone hadn't told her to turn the volume down.

She played around with the food some more, before forcing herself to look into his face. 'Okay. Let's do it your way and get the niceties over with. What are you doing these days? Still living in Rome, I suppose?'

'Not any more. These days I have an apartment in New York.'

'Oh?'

'You sound surprised.'

'Not really. Surprise would imply a degree of interest, which I simply don't have.' She pushed her plate away and—forgetting her no-carbs rule—started nibbling on a piece of bread instead. 'It's just that you used to act as though paradise was a place in Italy, sandwiched in between Umbria and Emilia Romagna.'

'My love of my homeland has not diminished, Justina,' he said silkily. 'And I go home whenever I can—though that is becoming increasingly less these days.'

'Business is doing well?' She made the question sound as if it was a bore to have to ask it.

He attempted a modest shrug, but she reflected with a growing feeling of frustration that modesty was one of the few things he didn't do well.

'Business is doing excellently. We've expanded our interests in North America and I love the vibrancy of New York. Okay, it isn't Tuscany—but you can't have everything.'

Justina ate some more bread—as if that could help

fill the emotional hole which Dante had exposed with his words. She didn't want to think about Tuscany—or the *palazzo* where the D'Arezzo family had lived for centuries. She had been blown away by the dramatic beauty of the region and the country itself, but her visit there hadn't been a success. Actually, that was a complete understatement. Dante's aristocratic family had disapproved of his English pop-star fiancée—especially as her visit had coincided with the release of a promotional video. The one where she'd been dancing energetically while not wearing a bra. Even she had been appalled by how *raunchy* the finished product had appeared to be—but it wouldn't have seemed very credible for her to come out and say so at the time.

She had been deemed an unsuitable girlfriend for one of the D'Arezzo men, as well as being a potentially bad influence on his younger sister, and their trip had been cut abruptly short. At the time Justina had accepted what had seemed a rather harsh verdict because she'd had no choice other than to accept it. But it had been yet another nail in the coffin of their relationship.

'Can't have everything?' she echoed sarcastically. 'But I thought you were the man who always believed he could. Who made "having it all" into an art form!'

'Oh, how *brittle* you sound, Justina,' he murmured. 'I do hope that your attitude isn't motivated by envy or avarice. Career taken a nose-dive, has it?'

She was tempted to tell him to go to hell, but some remnant of pride stopped her. *Let him know that you've carved a respectable life for yourself,* she thought. That the sacrifices she'd made had been worth it. She was independent and *proud* of it. *And she was never going to be like her mother.*

'On the contrary, I'm living in London and still writing songs,' she said. 'But for other people now.'

'And you're successful?'

'Oh, I do okay.' Justina kept her smile tight. She could have told him about her recent chart-topping song, or the invitation to write the score for an upcoming musical, but he wouldn't be impressed. Dante didn't approve of ambition unless it came from a man. 'It keeps me in shoes.'

'Very expensive shoes, by the look of them.' He lowered his gaze to study her skyscraper heels before lifting his head to let his eyes drift lazily over her face. And it was still the most beautiful face he had ever seen. Her pink lips were pressed together as if she was trying to decide what to do with them and Dante felt a rush of pure and potent lust. It hit his skin like the buffeting of a powerful wave. It turned the blood in his veins into a heated flow as he imagined kissing her again.

And in that moment he knew that he was going to have her one last time. That this fever wouldn't go away unless he did. He realised then that his desire for her was like a disease which had lain dormant all these years and the sight of her had suddenly reactivated it all over again.

He felt the heavy aching at his groin as he leaned

forward a little. 'And what about men?' he questioned softly.

'Men?'

His gaze was steady; his voice was not quite. 'Nobody in your life you like enough to bring him along today as your "plus one"?'

Justina met the blaze of his eyes, determined he wouldn't discover the truth. Because wouldn't he laugh—or, even worse, act *smug*—if he knew that her time with him had ruined her for other men? That she'd been unable to trust another man enough to get close to—even if she'd found anyone else attractive enough to want to try.

So why not play games with him? Why not pretend that she loved men just as they loved her? Surely pride demanded something along those lines? For Dante was traditional and old-fashioned enough to see her still-single status as some kind of failure.

She took another sip of wine. 'Oh, I do all right with men,' she said, and the sudden darkening of his face gave her a brief thrill of pleasure. Because if that was *jealousy* then it was only a fraction of what she'd felt when she'd walked into his hotel suite that day and seen that naked woman writhing all over him. Fighting back a sudden feeling of nausea, she raised her eyebrows, as if daring him to continue his interrogation.

'But nobody permanent?' he persisted.

'Nope.' She made it sound like a conscious choice instead of an unwanted situation into which she had been cast. She hadn't realised that love would be so difficult to find second time around. She hadn't realised that she would look at other men, compare them to the arrogant Tuscan—and be left completely cold. 'I don't do permanence. And now, if you don't mind, Dante, I think we've exhausted pretty much everything we need to say to each other.'

Very deliberately, she turned her back on him and started talking to the Brigadier, who was sitting on her other side—although it took her a moment before she had composed herself enough to concentrate. But the old soldier was a lucky choice of companion. He knew lots about the groom's ancestral home, and once he got going there was no stopping him. Acting like balm on her ruffled senses, he made for unexpectedly engaging company—especially to someone like Justina, who'd had such an erratic education.

Her mother's louche and nomadic lifestyle had meant that Justina had changed schools as often as most people changed their wardrobes. By the age of seventeen she'd had a wealth of experience, but not much in the way of formal teaching—unless you counted her mother's weekly master classes in gold-digging. But from an early age she'd learnt the art of asking the right questions, and the Brigadier was able to answer them all to her satisfaction. He told her all about the battles which had been fought around the beautiful Norfolk estate, and described in detail all the house's treasures—including the rare Titian painting in the picture gallery.

If only she could have blocked out the occasional drift of Dante's accent as she heard him entertaining his side of the table throughout the meal. The redhead wearing emeralds had a particularly piercing laugh, and Justina had to stop herself from wincing every time she heard it. If only she could have blotted out her aching awareness of his presence, too. She could almost feel the heat from his body and detect the raw, masculine scent which was so uniquely his.

Someone began banging a spoon against the side of a glass, and as the bride's father stood up to make his speech Dante leaned over to speak in her ear.

'You turned your back on me, Justina—and nobody ever does that.'

'Shh. I know you love talking about yourself but you really must be quiet. The speeches are about to begin.' She caught the brief look of frustration on his face, before sitting back in her seat and fixing her eyes on the top table.

The bride's father began to speak. his crumpled linen suit and long hair making him stand out from the rest of the guests. He told a few inappropriate anecdotes which should have had the aristocratic relatives groaning—but it was such a happy occasion that people just started giggling in response. Justina looked around at all the laughing faces and a terrible emptiness started to gnaw away at her. Suddenly it felt as if everyone was sitting within the warm circle of a fire while she was alone on the outskirts, in the dark and cold. The outsider who had no real sense of belonging. And hadn't it always been that way?

She sat through the rest of the speeches and laughed in all the right places, but after the ceremonial cutting of the cake she picked up her satin clutch-bag and looked around. Dante was busy talking to the redhead and she doubted whether the Brigadier would miss her too much. She'd make as if she was going to the washroom and leave without anybody noticing. She'd have the early night she needed and sleep away her jet-lag—and tomorrow she would wake up and start forgetting about Dante all over again.

She managed to slip from the room without comment, but had got no further than the pillared entrance hall when her search to locate her cell phone was halted by the deep caress of a familiar accent.

'Going somewhere?'

She turned to find Dante effectively blocking her path, and she hated the shiver which whispered its way down over her spine. Hated even more the way she seemed mesmerised by the sardonic curve of his lips. 'Trying to,' she said pointedly. 'If you'd be so good as to get out of my way?'

'But there's dancing.'

'I know there is. But I've had enough.' *Of you.* She didn't say the words out loud; she didn't need to.

He frowned. 'So you're travelling back to London?'

'Not tonight, no. I've booked into a hotel in Burnham Market.' She gave a little sigh as she met his raised eyebrows. 'It's a town not far from here.'

He nodded as he delved into the pocket of his suit trousers for his car keys. 'I'll drive you there.'

'Thanks, but I'd prefer to get a cab.'

'Don't be melodramatic, Justina. A cab will take ages and my car is parked by the stables.'

In the cool shadows she could see the bright gleam of his eyes.

'What are you so afraid of?'

She wondered how he would react if she told him the truth. She was afraid of wanting him. Of wanting him to kiss her, despite knowing that it was wrong. Because what did it say about *her* that she should still desire him after everything that had happened?

'I'd hate to drag you away from the party.'

'I'm happy to be dragged. As it happens, I'd intended driving back to London tonight anyway—I have a flight to the States tomorrow.'

Put like that, it made her continued resistance sound unreasonable—or maybe she just didn't have the strength to oppose him any more.

Justina accompanied him outside as he handed his keys to a valet. While they were waiting for his car to be brought round he turned to her.

'Whatever happened to Lexi?' he asked suddenly.

Justina met his curious gaze. It was a long time since anyone had mentioned Alexi Gibson, the third member of the Lollipops—or 'Sexy Lexi' as the press used to dub her.

'You know she went solo?' she questioned. 'That it was her desire to go it alone which led to the break-up of the band?'

'No, I didn't know that.' Up until the day he'd received the wedding invitation he'd deliberately excised all references to the Lollipops from his life, as carefully as a surgeon might remove an area of diseased tissue. 'Is she here?'

'Nope. Nobody ever sees her since she married one of Hollywood's biggest players.' Briefly, Justina found herself wondering if Lexi was happy—and for the first time in a long time, she turned the question on herself. Am *I* happy? she wondered. The answer hit her with a jolt. She wasn't. Successful and fairly contented, yes—and certainly fulfilled in her choice of career. But happy? No way. Not compared to the happiness she'd known in the past, with Dante.

The valet had arrived with Dante's sports car—a low and gleaming machine which made wriggling into the passenger seat something of a challenge, despite the accommodating side-split in her cheongsam dress.

'Name of hotel?' he questioned steadily, as if the sight of her bare thigh hadn't just sent his blood pressure shooting through the ceiling.

'The Smithsonian.'

She watched as he keyed the details into his satnav and then sat back as the powerful car pulled away from the big house with a small spurt of gravel. The silence which descended hung heavily on the air—with what they *weren't* talking about filling the space around them and making the atmosphere feel claustrophobic. The elephant in the room was alive and well, thought Justina wryly, and currently crammed into a powerful car in Norfolk.

They drew up outside the lighted hotel which stood in a pretty Georgian Square and her fingers were unsteady as she tried to unclip her seat belt. Despite her relief that the awkward journey was over, she felt strangely reluctant to get out and just walk away. It was funny, but the older you got, the more you realised the significance of goodbyes. At twenty-five she hadn't really thought about whether or not she'd see Dante again because at that age she hadn't been thinking beyond her heartbreak. This time she was aware that their paths were unlikely to cross again, that this was probably the last time she would ever see him—and she was unprepared for the sudden twist of pain in her heart.

'Justina?'

The soft dip in his voice was distracting, and so was the false intimacy created by the limited space inside the vehicle. In the dim light she could see the gleam of his eyes and she became aware of just how close he was. 'What?'

There was a pause. 'You know that I still want you.'

She thought how *blatant* he was. How only Dante D'Arezzo would have the nerve to come out and say something like that. 'Well, tough. The feeling isn't mutual.'

'Oh, come on. You've been undressing me with your eyes since you walked down the aisle and saw me at the cathedral.'

'I think you must be mistaken. I'm not interested in a man who spreads his favours so thinly.'

There was a heartbeat of a pause, and when he spoke his voice was harsh. 'You know damned well that it was over when I went with her! How many times do I have to tell you that?'

Justina looked down at her lap. Yes, it had been over between them—certainly as far as he'd been concerned. Her determination to go on tour with the Lollipops had led to Dante abruptly ending their engagement. But she had missed him. She had missed him more than she'd thought it possible to miss anyone. The reality of life without him had hit her hard, and his absence had felt like falling down a bottomless black hole. So she had flown back to England unexpectedly, planning to go to his hotel and ask him if they could try again, to give it one more go—because deep down she'd thought that they loved one another enough to overcome their fundamental differences. But she had been cruelly mistaken.

Her last memory of Dante was bursting into his hotel suite and seeing him in bed. But he hadn't been alone. His eyes had been closed and something had been moving at his groin beneath the sheet. Justina's horrified gasp had made the movement stop and a head had emerged. It had been a tousled blond head, and somehow that had only driven the knife in deeper. As if he was piling on cliché after cliché. Not just taking another lover—taking a *blonde* lover.

Justina had managed to turn on her heel and make it all the way to the lift. She'd even managed to hold it together enough to hail a taxi outside the hotel. But her heart had felt as if he'd stamped on it with a metal-studded boot.

She had cut all communication with him from that moment and done everything she could to try to forget him. No one could have been more assiduous than Justina in cutting all references to Dante from her life. She had destroyed every photo of him and had sold all the jewellery he had showered on her and then donated the proceeds to charity.

She was aware that his dark eyes were still fixed on her questioningly, and she vowed that he would never know the true depths of her heartbreak. 'I wasn't expecting you to move on with quite such insulting speed!'

'You think I should have waited?' he questioned heatedly. 'When already you had kept me waiting for so long? Waiting while you did your world tour. Waiting while you did more of your television interviews and your damned newspaper spreads. You knew the kind of man I was, Justina. I was young and I was hungry and I expected the woman I loved to be by my side, supporting me. I had certain *appetites* which needed to be fed—and I could not tolerate the life you were forcing me to lead. Our very separate lives.'

'It's done,' she said flatly, her heart contracting painfully as she heard him say it. *The woman I loved.* Past tense. The love was gone—for both of them. 'It's in the past, Dante—and it was best for everyone in the long run. It certainly made for a clean break.'

His eyes searched her face and in that moment he felt a pang of regret washing over him. Guilt, too. And he was unprepared for the way it made his heart clench, as if someone was squeezing it with icy fingers. 'You know, you were never meant to find me with her,' he said. 'I'm sorry if I hurt you.'

Justina nodded. Once she would have given anything to have him acknowledge the pain he'd caused. But now it sounded like a patronising afterthought. Almost as if he suspected that she'd never really been able to move on from him without this final sense of closure.

And yet was that so far from the truth? Despite all her best intentions she'd never really got over him, had she? Part of her was still stuck inside her old self, still remembering the lover he'd been—against whom all subsequent men had been measured only to fail.

Maybe she had continued to idealise him. Maybe his undeniable qualities as a lover had made her place him on an impossibly high pedestal which had subsequently distorted her views on men. Was that what had caused her to erect these high barriers around herself, which nobody else had ever been able to scale?

Pride helped her form careless words, and a career on the stage meant that she was able to utter them with a degree of conviction. 'The hurt I felt was just a part of growing up,' she said. 'You were simply a necessary part of my sexual education, Dante.'

For a moment there was a stunned silence, and when he spoke his voice was underpinned with a dark note of anger. 'I must say that I've heard myself described in many ways—but never quite like that before.' The tip of his tongue slowly traced the outline of his upper lip. 'And did I provide you with good grades during this sexual *education* I gave you?'

Justina's heart skipped a beat as her body began to ache with half-forgotten hunger. She told herself she ought to get out of the car while she still had a chance, but it was as if someone had turned her limbs to stone. 'I don't…I don't remember.'

'You don't? That's such a pity. Then maybe I ought to refresh your memory for you.'

She met the challenge in his shadowed eyes and saw the way his lips had parted. Did she murmur something—or indicate with her expression that she wasn't averse to the idea? Was that what made him move closer?

And suddenly they were kissing. Kissing as she'd forgotten how to. His hands were at her waist and she was reaching for his shoulders. In no time at all he was running his fingers over her satin-covered breasts and she was moaning like a woman in pain.

He snapped his seat belt free, swiftly followed by hers, but the space inside the car was cramped and already the windows were starting to get steamed up. It was hard to move, because there was nowhere *to* move, and her cheongsam made it even harder. The realisation that they were sitting right outside her hotel didn't even enter the equation until she heard Dante mutter something urgent in Italian. He dragged his mouth away from hers and she could see the look of frustration burning in his eyes.

'Not here,' he bit out, shaking his dark head. 'Not like this. Take me inside, Justina.' He bent his head to drift his lips over hers. 'Take me into your body before I explode.'

CHAPTER THREE

HER HOTEL ROOM was pristinely tidy. It was one of the things which Dante remembered as being uniquely Justina. While the rest of the band had existed in a rubble of half-eaten room service food and discarded wine bottles she had lived in her own neat little bubble, sitting writing her songs in the middle of all the chaos. He remembered her telling him that it was her particular antidote to a messy and erratic upbringing.

But his thoughts about her orderliness lasted for about as long as it took for the door to close behind them, for him to take her into his arms again and for his mouth to crush down on hers in another hungry kiss. He could feel the restless movement of her body as she writhed against him, but he got the sense that her mind was screaming out all kinds of objections.

Very deliberately, he grazed his mouth over hers with a slow and erotic brush. 'I want you,' he said, his words coming out unsteadily. 'I have never wanted a woman as much as I want you in this moment.'

Justina closed her eyes as his lips moved to her neck,

her fingers tangling themselves luxuriously in the thick darkness of his hair. 'Dante…' she whispered, knowing that the rest of the sentence went something like, *You know we shouldn't be doing this.* But the words remained unspoken—and how could they be spoken when he had started touching her breasts like that?

'What the hell kind of dress is this?' he questioned as he felt around for a zip.

'It's called a…a cheongsam. I…I bought it in Singapore and I—'

'I'm not interested in its history!' Roughly, he cut through her stumbling explanation. 'The only thing I'm interested in is how to get the damned thing off.'

'There are buttons down the side,' she gasped.

'*Sono mille!*' His fingers were trembling as he began to fumble them open. 'How many?'

She felt cool air rushing onto her skin and told herself to call a halt to this madness. But she couldn't. She just *couldn't.* Her body was too hungry, her desire too strong to be able to resist what he was doing to her. Hadn't she spent the past five years wondering if she'd ever feel like this again? Wondering if her body would ever feel this incomparable rush of desire? And suddenly Justina knew that she didn't want to be passive. That if this was to be their swansong then they would come together as the equals they'd never really been. She was no longer the virgin lover he had needed to teach. She had graduated with honours, and maybe it was time to remember just how much she'd loved having sex with this man.

She kicked off her high heels and sent them flying across the room before beginning to tug at his tie.

'Impatient?' he queried, thinking that in the past she would have slid the shoes tidily from her feet.

'Aren't you?' she whispered back as she turned her attention to his shirt. She slid open the buttons and greedily peeled it away to reveal the honed torso beneath, bending her head to graze her teeth against his skin, her tongue licking luxuriously against its silken surface.

'*Dio.*' He shuddered, and tore at another button of her dress. He pulled the garment away from her with hands which were shaking, and if such a reaction was unheard of for someone of his experience he didn't care. He unclipped her bra in one deft movement. Her panties he disposed of by ripping apart the delicate lace with his fingers, and he heard her little gasp of pleasure as they brushed over her honeyed heat.

'You always liked me to play a little rough, didn't you, *tesoro*?' he demanded as he tugged off the last of his own clothing—and was taken off guard by her fervent passion as she pushed him down onto the bed.

She moved over him, her face filled with an expression he could never remember seeing before as she straddled him. Her eyes were slitted so he couldn't read them, and she was biting her lips as if she was trying to stop them from trembling.

'Do it,' he commanded.

But Justina shook her head. Tonight *she* was going to call the shots. This was going to be her therapy, the recovery she needed. She would feast on his body until she'd had her fill. She would let the harsh light of reality shine down on this demi-god of her imagination and by morning she would see him for the mortal he really was. This was *sex*, she told herself fiercely—and she wasn't going to make the mistake of confusing it with love.

'I'll *do it* when I'm good and ready.'

Dante moaned as she circled her hips to brush her feminine core over his steely erection so that he could almost feel her—but not quite. She was close enough for him to be able to plunge inside her, and yet she kept her moist treasure almost tantalisingly out of reach. His head fell back against the pillow and for a moment he felt almost helpless. This was not how he liked it to happen—at least not with Justina. He liked to be in control, to play the dominant role, and yet she was writhing around on top of him like some teasing whore. And, God help him, he *liked* it.

'*Per favore,*' he groaned. '*Please.*'

His heartfelt plea made something inside her snap, and despite revelling in her fleeting moment of power Justina knew she couldn't wait any longer. Positioning herself, she slid down and slowly took his hard, silken length deep into her body. She heard him groan as he filled her and for a moment she couldn't move. She wanted to fall against him. To collapse against his chest and hug him, clinging tightly as if she would never let him go. To tell him that nothing had ever felt as good as this and nothing ever would. But she wasn't going to be passive, was she? Or weak. She was going to enjoy her body and make the most out of a situation she had never thought would happen.

Nor should it be happening, taunted a mocking voice in her head, but she shut the door on it as she began to move. Their warm bodies met and reacquainted themselves as she eased his throbbing shaft in and out of her eager flesh. She groaned as he played with her breasts, and when his thumb began to rub against her clitoris she flung her head back and gave a low and shuddering cry. It felt so amazing that she never wanted it to stop, but it didn't last as long as she wanted it to. How could it, when they were both so close to the edge? She tried to prolong the erotic dance for as long as possible, but the hot waves were too powerful to hold back. Dark impulses danced over her skin as she gripped his shoulders and pushed her hips forward, driving him in right up to the hilt.

'Justina!' he gasped.

'Dante!' she moaned in response as she felt the first shimmering tugs hovering at the edge of her consciousness—and then, as she began to go under, he flipped her onto her back, his powerful body dark and tense as he drove into her with increasing speed. Her body felt as if it was exploding with pleasure as the first of the spasms hit her, and then she heard him give his own ragged cry as his head sank down against her neck.

Justina kept her eyes tightly shut as their bodies gradually grew still and felt a brief pang of melancholy wash over her. But she was damned if she was going to let it show. She wasn't going to start dwelling on how amazing it had been because that was nothing new. And she wasn't going to start wishing that they could go back to what they'd had before. Because they couldn't, could they? You could never go back.

Even if you could she wouldn't want to—not with Dante. *Especially* not with Dante. Because he was bad news. Or had she forgotten that? Had the urgent greed of her body made her conveniently push away the bitter truth? He'd hurt her more than she'd thought it was possible to hurt and he had the power to do it still. And he would. She knew that. She knew all about the complex factors which motivated him. She knew that he'd seen some of her behaviour as humiliation to his macho pride, and perhaps this was his way of getting even. Taking her body with careless disregard for her feelings.

She wriggled a little, aware that they were still locked intimately together. He was sleeping—or at least he seemed to be doing a good impression of sleeping, with the dark arcs of his long lashes feathering his sculpted cheeks. Once there would have been love as she looked at him, but that emotion had been replaced by a mixture of anger and regret. How could she have done that? How *could* she? She'd brought him up here to her hotel room and just had sex with him—without any of the usual preliminaries. And why, of all the men in all the world, did it have to be *him* and only him who could make her feel like this? The only man she'd ever been intimate with was the man who had hurt her. Who had destroyed her trust completely.

She felt him stir inside her. She felt his burgeoning erection and remembered how deliciously *insatiable* he'd used to be. Once he would have lowered his head to kiss her and started to make love to her all over again. But she wasn't going to let that happen. *Please give me the strength to push him away,* she prayed—but Dante got there first.

His silent withdrawal from her sticky body seemed fraught with symbolism—all of it dark. He hadn't said a single word, and the silence in the room seemed to be growing bigger by the second. He was levering himself up onto one elbow and appeared to be viewing her as dispassionately as a scientist might look into a petrie dish, to see what rogue organisms had sprung up overnight.

'That was some sex,' he said, and Justina met the cold expression in his eyes.

She kept her own response deliberately light. *Don't let him know how you feel. Hide your hurt, your anger and your shame and be the kind of woman he usually ends up in bed with. Casual. No-strings.* She even managed to curve her lips into the faintest of smiles. 'You liked it?'

Dante's face darkened. 'I'm sure you don't need me to tell you how good you are.' He paused and his voice took on an empty, hollow quality. 'I'd forgotten quite how good.'

But he had never known her quite like that before, he realised. And, despite his own very comprehensive love life since they'd parted, he felt sick at the thought of her doing the same. He tried to tell himself that it was a *good* thing to realise that she'd changed. That she was no longer the sweet innocent he'd initiated into sex. He hadn't expected her to be, had he? *Had* he?

'I expect you've learnt a lot from all the other men you've known in the interim,' he said.

Justina gave her naked shoulders a little wriggle. 'I always make it a rule not to discuss other lovers when I'm in bed with a man. It strikes me as particularly bad manners.'

Her words made his mouth harden and he pushed back the rumpled bedclothes before getting out of bed. She watched as he headed for the bathroom, just as she'd watched him do so many times before. His naked olive body was magnificent, the perfect globes of his paler buttocks contrasting with the dark musculature of his powerful thighs.

He emerged minutes later and without another word reached for his clothes and began getting dressed.

'Going?' she questioned, still in that same studiedly casual voice.

He paused in the act of pulling on his shirt, his dark

eyes flicking over her with a look which was half lust, half disgust. 'I have a flight to the States in the morning. I told you that.'

'Of course.' She didn't want him to think that she minded him leaving so she got out of bed herself, reaching for the silk robe which was lying neatly folded on the chair by the bed. 'Would you like a drink before you go?' she questioned. 'I can ring down for coffee if you like. It's a long drive back to London.'

A dark spear of jealousy lanced through him. Dante wondered if she knew how *seasoned* she sounded. As if she asked men that kind of question most days of the week. He saw her slide the slippery robe over her luscious nakedness and quickly averted his eyes. Maybe she did.

'No, thanks.'

Justina began pulling the pins from her mussed-up hair and shaking it free. 'Is there something particular in New York?' she questioned. 'Something which can't wait?'

He curled his tie into a gleaming coil and slid it into his jacket pocket. 'There's a big party I don't want to miss.'

'Oh?' He might as well have been talking about the stock market for all the emotion she put into her next question. 'Something special?'

Dante looked at her. Her hair was now free of all the pins and had tumbled down around her shoulders and she was brushing it. It wasn't as long as he remembered, but it was still thick and raven-dark. It made her look like some beautiful dark angel, he thought, and for a moment he wanted to kiss her again, to ravage her. To tumble her back down on the bed and thrust right into her all over again until he had emptied himself inside her. But he couldn't. Or rather, he wouldn't. Because while once had been a mistake, twice would be insanity. They were too different. They always had been.

He shrugged. 'Just a party.'

'Oh?' Justina fought against the instinct which was telling her to leave it alone and instead let her finger hover over the self-destruct button. 'Whose?'

'A girl's.'

Beneath her silk robe Justina felt her skin ice to goose bumps. Had he…had he done it again? Taken her to bed when he was in a relationship with someone else? Her heart felt as cold as her skin, but somehow she managed another of those light smiles—as if they'd just done nothing more daring than enjoy a cup of tea together, instead of romping wildly on the bed. Because she was *not* going to fall to pieces.

'Well, drive carefully,' she said. 'And I hope you have a safe journey back to America.'

Dante's mouth twisted. How dismissive she sounded. As if what they'd done had meant nothing. Because it *had* meant nothing, he reminded himself bitterly. They both knew that.

His mind began to play back an erotic tape of what had just happened. Justina straddling him. Justina riding him. The way he'd ridden her back until that sweet release had claimed them both. The forbidden ache of sex throbbed thickly through his veins and in that moment of renewed desire he despised himself almost as much as he despised her for what they had done.

But not enough to stop him from pulling her into his arms and lowering his lips to a mouth which was now closed and resisting. A couple of seconds was all it took for that resistance to vanish, for her lips to part again and allow his tongue to slip inside. A couple of seconds more and she was kissing him right back, her fingers tangling in his hair the way they always did when she was turned on. If he'd given it any longer he suspected that he could have taken her again—right there on the floor on which they stood. He suspected that if he slid one finger between her legs he could make her come in seconds, the way he'd always been able to do. And wasn't he tempted to do just that? *Wasn't* he?

But Justina was pushing at his chest with two balled-up fists and tearing her mouth from his. Her eyes were dark with anger as she took a few unsteady steps away from him, and her breathing was ragged as she struggled to control it.

'You've got what you came for—now get out of here,' she snapped, because never in her life had she felt so *used*. 'Go back to New York and get the hell out of my life.'

For a moment they stared at one another as rage and

desire simmered in the air around them, and then Dante picked up his jacket and slung it over his shoulder.

'Goodbye, Justina,' he said, and the smile which curved his lips was bitter. 'Thanks for the memory.'

CHAPTER FOUR

THE NIGHTMARE COULDN'T possibly get any worse.

It just couldn't.

As warm, fat raindrops teemed from the sky Justina hurried into a shop on the busy Singaporean street as fast as her bulky frame would allow—but it wasn't easy. The huge swell of her baby made movement difficult, especially in the sultry heat which characterised this vibrant city. A minute was all it had taken for her to get soaked right through, and now she stood shivering as the icy blast of the shop's air-conditioning blasted over her damp skin.

Trying to conceal her shape behind a rack of designer clothes, she peered out through the blur of rain. People were hastily putting up their umbrellas. Others were standing huddled beneath bus shelters as they sought to avoid the daily spectacle of the tropical storm. Nobody seemed to be looking in her direction. Nobody at all.

Justina swallowed down the sudden dryness in her throat. Was she simply going crazy—imagining that someone was following her? That another photographer planned to leap out to take a picture? She couldn't understand why the press were so interested in the fact that she was having a baby when loads of women had babies out of wedlock these days without stigma.

Yet she couldn't deny the media interest—especially since the Lollipops *Sweetest Hits* had been re-released just before Roxy's wedding and had stormed up the charts all over the world. She still had a public profile, which had become higher as a result of those renewed sales. On days where there wasn't a lot of news around she could still sometimes find one of those rather depressing pieces about 'unlucky in love' Justina Perry hidden in the back pages of the newspapers—the ones which wondered why she was still single.

Only now she had given them an even bigger story— *STILL SINGLE AND NOW EXPECTING! WHO'S THE MYSTERY FATHER, JUSTINA?*

After she'd gone through the first stages of dismay and denial, she had tried to conceal her pregnancy for as long as possible—and when that had become out of the question she had stayed out of the limelight as much as she could. But the press were like hungry dogs. One sniff of a juicy story and they came looking. Lately there'd been a whole spate of articles speculating about the identity of her baby's father—she was just praying that nobody had seen her disappearing from Roxy's wedding with Dante D'Arezzo. That was the kind of snippet which would find its way into a gossip column, forever linking her name to the Italian billionaire.

'Can I get you a chair, ma'am?'

Justina turned round to find a shop assistant regarding her with concern. Perhaps she was worried that the tired-looking Englishwoman was about to give birth in the middle of her shop and it wasn't really Justina's role to reassure her that she wasn't due for another five weeks.

'No, thanks. I'm fine. I'll take a cab back to my hotel. The rain looks as if it's stopping now.'

'You're sure, ma'am?'

'Yes, thank you.' From somewhere, she summoned up a smile. 'Quite sure.'

But during her shivering journey back to Raffles Hotel, where she always stayed when she was in the city, Justina couldn't seem to halt the thoughts which seemed determined to keep any peace of mind at bay. Round and round in her head went the indisputable truth. She was pregnant with Dante's baby and terrified he would find out.

Distractedly, she rubbed at her temples. He was bad news. He was a player. He was everything that was dangerous in a man—especially where she was concerned. He had taken her to bed and soared with her to the stars before they crashed back down to earth again. And she couldn't just blame Dante for what had happened, because she had been culpable, too. She'd practically ripped his clothes off and ravished him, despite all the terrible history between them.

She felt the sudden clench of her heart, but it was

more with anger than with pain. She had been head-strong and stupid. She had given in to desire without thinking about the consequences and that's why she found herself in this position. But there was *no way* she was going to go running to him. Not when he'd made it clear that what had happened had been a re-grettable one-off.

She kept telling herself that interest would die down if she kept her counsel. She lived the kind of interna-tional life where it was perfectly acceptable to be vague about the identity of her baby's father. The people she wrote songs for wouldn't have cared if the devil himself had claimed paternity. The only person who was really interested was the London doctor whose care she was under—and he wasn't making any moral judgements. That was the sum total of people it really affected. She certainly wasn't relying on any help from her mother, whose reaction to the news had been entirely predict-able—if a little sad.

'I'm not ready to be a grandmother!' Elaine Perry had snapped, not seeming to notice Justina's white-faced response.

Justina had stared at the woman with whom she had such a complicated relationship. Her once-beautiful mother, who was unable to accept that her looks were now fading and who tried to compensate for that by slapping on far too much make-up. 'But, Mum—'

'Don't "Mum" me! If you think I'm spending my time knitting bootees or acting as an unpaid babysitter, then you're mistaken, Justina.' A coy smile had followed as the older woman had fiddled with hair which was growing thinner by the year. 'I *do* still have a busy social life of my own, you know.'

And Justina, feeling sick for all kinds of reasons, had not responded. What compassion could she expect from a woman whose life had been spent as mistress to a series of wealthy men she'd milked for every penny she could? Who was now reduced to living with some creepy and aging *roué* in the centre of Paris?

Justina still felt shaky as her cab drew up outside the hotel and she went inside to collect her key from the desk in the spacious lobby. The atmosphere of the iconic hotel usually had a soothing effect on her. The faded brocade chairs and tall potted palms always made her think of a more elegant time, and whenever she stayed there she felt part of it. Only today the magic of Raffles wasn't working. She felt as if she was on a tiny raft, bobbing around in an unforgiving sea, with no real place to go and drop anchor.

Maybe she needed the restorative power of a deep bath and a strong cup of tea, and then she would—

'Justina.'

Someone was saying her name in a way which only one person ever could. Disbelief made her skin turn to ice as she heard the voice which had haunted her waking thoughts and troubled dreams for the past seven and a half months. She shook her head in hopeful denial. She was imagining it. She *had* to be imagining it.

Slowly she turned to see the dark and forbidding figure of Dante D'Arezzo, and her heart began to flutter wildly in her chest. No. She wasn't imagining it. Nobody else spoke like that. And nobody else looked like that either. Dante was here in the flesh—vibrant with life and looking immaculate in cool, pale linen, his face an intimidating study of dark fury as his gaze seared into her.

The angled slant of his cheekbones cast shadows over his features and his mouth was grim and unsmiling. She had never seen his powerful body look quite so tense. The only thing about him which moved was a little muscle which was flickering at his temple. For a moment she swayed with the sheer shock of seeing him, but maybe he'd anticipated that kind of reaction for his hand reached out towards her. Strong fingers clamped around her forearm to steady her, and she could feel the burning warmth of his flesh digging into her icy skin. And God forgive her but her body instantly thrilled to that touch, even though it was more the touch of a captor than a lover. She could feel her shivering response to him, and she wondered if he could feel it, too.

'What…what are you doing here?' she demanded shakily as his brilliant gaze scorched through her.

Dante's heart began to accelerate with anger as he looked into her white face. What did she *think* he was doing here? Doing a leisurely tour of the Far East and bumping into her quite by chance? Did she imagine he was going to ask her to the bar to join him for one of the hotel's famous Singapore Slings?

'You and I need to talk,' he said grimly.

Justina bit her lip as distracted, crazy thoughts began to rush into her head. What if she called out and told the staff that she was being harassed? Wouldn't that sound bad, coming from a heavily pregnant woman? Wouldn't he instantly be ejected from the hotel, and probably from the country itself?

She wasn't so sure that he would. Dante could smooth-talk his way through most things. She could imagine him turning the full force of his charm on hotel security and managing to convince them that it was her *hormones* at work. And when it all boiled down to it her hormones *were* the only reason he was here. He wasn't here because he missed her or because he wanted her back in his bed. He wanted to speak to her about something which was glaringly obvious to both of them and she must accede to his wishes. She owed him that much, at least.

'Not here,' she said, her throat so dry that her words sounded strangled. 'We can go and have coffee in the Writers' Bar and—'

'No,' he snapped, imperiously cutting through her suggestion. 'I don't intend to have this conversation while you play to the crowd, Justina. Take me to your room.' He saw the brief look which hovered in her eyes and his mouth twisted with derision as he lowered his voice to a deadly hiss. 'Oh, please don't worry that I'm about to seduce you. Because let me assure you that's the last thing on my mind right now. In fact, let me put it even more plainly, just so that we can be very clear about where we stand. If you and I were alone on a desert island I think I'd gladly embrace celibacy rather than risk coming within two feet of you, you manipulative little bitch.'

The vitriol in his voice made Justina's hand fly to her lips in horror as she looked at him. Did he really hate her that much? But even if he did he had no right to talk to her that way. She was carrying a baby beneath her heart, and even if he wished it wasn't *his* baby it was certainly *her* baby, and she would defend it with every ounce of strength in her body.

So stop letting him intimidate you. Have the talk he wants—the talk you know you owe him.

Because wasn't this what she had been expecting—and dreading—for months? Wasn't this very meeting the reason why she'd taken on so many travelling commitments since discovering she was pregnant? Not daring to be in one place too long in case he found her, she had become a kind of bulky fugitive. A woman who was running away from the inevitable—only now the inevitable had caught up with her.

She shrugged. 'Okay. We'll talk. But it might be a good start if you stopped manhandling me like that.' Pointedly, she glanced down at the olive fingers which were still gripping her forearm, and then up into the hard gleam of his dark eyes. But the terrible thing was that she *liked* him touching her. For all his cruel words, and her fear of what he wanted, she liked the way he made her feel. And, shamefully, it was deprivation rather than relief which washed over her when he let her go, and her footsteps were a little unsteady as she turned and headed for the staircase.

Justina was aware of people watching them as they made their way from the public area of the hotel towards the residential part and guessed they must make a bizarre couple. She was all damp and bedraggled after being caught in the tropical storm, and Dante looked so indomitable as he shadowed her, his savagely beautiful face and powerful body making every female guest in the building glance at him twice.

In silence they walked towards her suite, and the dark gleam of the wooden verandas, the raffia furniture and the scent of flowers drifting up from the courtyard garden failed to calm Justina's mounting sense of anxiety. By the time she pushed open her door she felt like a piece of elastic which had been stretched so tightly that the faintest movement would violently snap it.

But she couldn't carry on feeling frayed and vulnerable like this. She had to stay in control and remember that she was dealing with a man for whom control was key. Some primitive part of her wanted to leave the door open—but she knew that the sound of their voices would carry and she couldn't risk that. With a heavy sigh of resignation, she closed it behind them.

'I need to use the bathroom,' she said.

It seemed almost too intimate a thing to say—which was a bizarre thought in the circumstances—but Justina needed to do more than relieve her pregnancy-weak bladder. Pride made her tug a brush through hair which was hanging down her back like rats' tails, and to slick on some pink lipstick which seemed to be the only colour in her white face.

She still needed to suck in a deep breath as she prepared to walk back in and face him. She felt sick with nerves—the way she'd used to feel just before she went out on stage—only this was much worse. On stage, her crippling fears had used to vanish the moment she heard the first chord of music and professionalism began to kick in. Today she had no idea how she was going to react to what lay ahead of her. These were new and uncharted waters—and she'd never seen anything more forbidding than the expression on Dante's dark face as she pushed open the door and walked into the lavish sitting room.

He was standing in front of the massive floor to ceiling windows which overlooked the veranda and yet somehow he made them look insignificant. His face was hard—like granite—and his eyes were cold as they flicked over the massive swell of her belly, as if he couldn't quite believe what he was seeing.

'You'd better sit down,' he said heavily.

She shook her head. *Damn* him for trying to act concerned. If he was so concerned then he wouldn't have leapt out at her like that, downstairs in the foyer. 'I'd prefer to stand,' she said.

For a moment Dante felt immense frustration shimmer over his skin. Wasn't that typical of Justina? So damned independent that she'd refuse to do the sensible thing. Even though her face looked as pale as flour, she was stubbornly refusing to sit down simply because *he* had been the one to suggest it.

'Have it your own way.'

'I intend to. How did you find me, Dante?'

'It wasn't difficult. You don't exactly blend into a crowd at the moment. I saw the erratic press reports about your…*condition*, and I worked out that the baby could be mine. I kept thinking that if that *were* the case you would contact me.' There was a pause and his eyes burned into her. 'I kept waiting for you to get in touch, and when you didn't I thought…'

His words tailed off. He'd thought that maybe he'd been mistaken, that it wasn't his baby at all. And hadn't the thought of *that* eaten him up with jealousy? The idea that he might have been just one in a line of men who had graced her bed? But the feeling hadn't left him, and neither had the strange *certainty* which had flooded through him. It had been certainty which had made him track her down. Which had made him board his private jet to Singapore, where he had been informed that she was staying alone in Raffles Hotel.

Intently, he stared at her, and he could feel the powerful beat of his heart thundering in his chest. The crazy thing was that he wanted to go over there and place the palm of his hand on her belly, as if to convince himself that this was real. And if he did that could he guarantee that the same dark hunger wouldn't flicker into life, the way it always did? Why was it that, no matter how much he tried to convince himself otherwise, he could never seem to stop wanting her?

'Is there something you need to tell me?'

Justina nodded as a wave of emotion threatened to overwhelm her, but somehow she held it back. *Don't act ashamed or intimidated,* she told herself. *Just deal with the facts.* But it was far from easy, because as she faced the accusation in his eyes a terrible yearning threatened to flare up inside her. She found herself wishing this could all have been different. That they were the same two people they'd once been—a couple in love who were planning to be together for the rest of their lives.

But it was not like that. It was nothing like that. Pointless to waste her time wishing that it was. *Pretend you're doing a television interview,* she told herself. *Act calmly. Take the emotion out of the subject and try not to turn this into a confrontation.*

Her voice was almost gentle. 'Is that a roundabout way of asking whether you're the father, Dante?'

CHAPTER FIVE

'AM I?' DANTE STARED at her, and his eyes had never looked colder than they did right then. 'Am I the father of your baby, Justina?'

For a moment she hesitated, tempted to tell him no. Because wouldn't that be easier all round? He could go back to New York and the life he'd made there. She would never have to see him again. *Never*. Financially— and hopefully emotionally—she could manage to be a good, single mother. Lots of women were.

But then she thought of the child she carried. The baby who was currently kicking beneath her fluttering heart as if it was trying out for a foetal football team. Could she wilfully deny her child the knowledge of its father just because that father didn't love *her*? Wouldn't that be the most selfish thing she could ever do—especially since she knew the pain and deprivation of growing up without a father? She knew how that could leave an empty hole which nothing could ever fill. She felt fiercely protective of this new life within her—and if she was being protective then that ruled out being selfish, didn't it? It might be better for *her* if Dante was out of her life, but it wouldn't be better for the baby.

'Yes,' she breathed—and then she said it again, so that there could be no going back. 'Yes, you are.'

For a moment he said nothing. He could hear the loud ticking of a clock as a surge of adrenalin flooded through him—his body automatically gearing itself up for fight or flight. He stared down at the elegant table beside him, on which stood a bowl of fruit so perfect that it might have been made from wax. For a split second he wanted to smash his fist through it. To see the apples disintegrating into pulp and the squashed oranges spurting out their juice. The desire was so strong that his big hands clenched into tight fists and he almost raised one. Until he forced himself to face facts as well as to re-exert the habitual control which had momentarily threatened to desert him.

Don't forget that this is a very single-minded woman, he told himself, as he stared into her wide amber eyes. *Who will do anything to get what she wants out of life.* He had witnessed her steely ambition first-hand. He had seen how she'd always put her career before him—it had been the main reason why he'd called off their wedding. So he needed to find out *all* the facts—not just the ones she had chosen to tell him.

'How can you be sure it's mine?'

Justina heard the rough challenge which distorted his voice. The question hurt—mainly because it sounded genuine and not asked simply as an attempt to insult her. Did he really think she behaved that way? Picked up men at weddings before taking them back to her room to have sex with them? She wondered how he would react if she told him that he was the only man she'd ever been intimate with, and that was how she knew he was the father. Would he laugh at her or simply pity her for spending the past five years without being able to move on?

'I just am,' she said flatly.

He shook his head. 'You'll have to do better than that.'

'What are you talking about?'

His mouth twisted. 'If you recall, you told me that you did "all right" with men.' He remembered the casual way she'd said it, and his own corresponding stab of jealousy. The overpowering sense of *darkness* which had shadowed his soul at the thought of other men making love to her the way he'd done. 'I got the distinct feeling that I wasn't the only one who shared your favours—not least from the enthusiastic way you climbed on top of me and ground those hips of yours so expertly against mine. I certainly didn't think that what happened between us on the night of the wedding was in any way unique.'

It was the cruellest thing he could have said, and Justina prayed that her face didn't register the hurt which was curling up inside her. He thought she was a tramp. He'd just come out and said so. 'Then why are you here if you believe that?' she questioned. 'Why this dramatic appearance—ambushing me in the lobby of my hotel as if you were in some kind of movie?'

'I'm here because I want the truth.'

'Why not just phone me up and ask me? Surely that would have been simpler for a man as busy as you?'

His gaze was steady. 'Would you have taken my call?'

Beneath his intense scrutiny, Justina shrugged. She wanted to save face. She wanted to hurt him back, as he had just hurt her. And instinctively she wanted to do the one thing she suspected would appal him so much that he might even contemplate going away and leaving her alone. She wanted to deny him. To let him know that she didn't need him. She wanted to offer him the freedom to walk away and leave her to face this on her own. 'Probably not,' she said eventually.

He nodded his head and turned to stare out of the window. Somehow it was easier to contemplate the courtyard gardens than continue to confront the fecund swell of her belly—though the white frangipani blossoms on the trees might as well have been lumps of snow for all the notice he took of them. But the brief respite was all he needed to regain his composure, and when he turned back he nodded.

'So it is true,' he said, his voice filled with silken venom. 'I have often been accused of cynicism, but even I couldn't believe that a woman could be quite so manipulative as you have been. It seems I was wrong.' There was a pause as his gaze raked over her, and even as the words formed on his lips he could feel the betraying leap of desire. 'You just wanted a stud, didn't you, Justina?'

'A stud?' Justina stared into eyes which resembled flat, dark metal. 'What…what are you talking about?'

His mouth twisted. 'I'm talking about the interview you gave just before Roxy's wedding. The one where you said how much you regretted not having had a baby and how much you'd like one.'

She heard the condemnatory tone which distorted his voice and for a moment felt vulnerable. Yes, she'd said that—but sometimes you said things which were only half-truths for all kinds of reasons. Especially when a journalist got you on the back foot. He *knew* that—and surely there was enough history between them for her to explain why she'd done it?

'Because that's what I felt I was *supposed* to say,' she defended. 'Because women who don't want babies are seen as monsters.'

'But I thought you *didn't* want babies.' His dark brows shot up. 'How could you possibly want them when your damned career was always so important to you and took precedence over everything else? You told me that there wasn't enough *time* in your life for children—and I can't see that having changed.'

Frustratedly, she shook her head. Hadn't he realised that at the time she'd said that it had been fear which had motivated her—as well as ambition? Her career had mattered to her because it had been a symbol of her own survival, as well as her success. She'd still been on the way up, and it had meant too much to her to simply let it slide just because that was what he wanted. But Dante had also wanted her pregnant as soon as they were married, and that had scared the hell out of her—and not just because she'd been so young. She had tried to explain that it was partly down to the awful experience she'd had with her own mother, which made her want to wait, but he had been immovable. Women married and then they became pregnant—it was as primitive as that to Dante.

'You don't understand, Dante.'

He shook his dark head and gave a cynical laugh. 'Oh, but I do, Justina. I understand only too well. You had sex with me—what? Five years after we'd last seen one another? Most women would have slapped my face for even trying it on. But not you. Oh, no. You wanted me from the moment that you saw me in the cathedral—I could read it in your eyes as clearly as if you'd come straight out and propositioned me.'

'I'm sorry if I don't match up to the saintlike status of your other lovers!'

'We didn't even use any protection!'

'I didn't realise that was solely the woman's responsibility.'

'I assumed you were still on the pill,' he snapped, knowing that he should have stopped to find out. But he hadn't. He hadn't cared about anything other than finding himself in the tight, molten slickness of her body again after so long. And hadn't it felt good? Hadn't it felt like *heaven*? He swallowed as he tried to force the erotic memory to the back of his mind—but he couldn't. It had been haunting him ever since—so how could he expect it to disappear when the woman who had so lured him was standing right in front of him? 'Why would you take such a risk with a man you were never likely to see again after that night?'

Justina stared into the cold condemnation on his face. Because she hadn't been thinking straight, that was why. So blinded by passion that common sense hadn't got a look-in. Oh, *why* did it have to be him who'd made her feel all these things? Why did he *still* make her feel them even now? If he walked across the room and started to kiss her, she honestly didn't know how she'd respond.

'You tell me,' she said tonelessly.

'Okay. I will.' His eyes grew hard and his voice was calculating—like a detective who was poised on the brink of a breakthrough. 'I'll tell you exactly how I think it was. Maybe you wanted a baby. You'd reached a time in your life where you realised you'd better get a move on if you wanted to be a mother. Only maybe you wanted a baby without all the added trouble of an accompanying man. Isn't that what every successful career woman craves these days, Justina? The designer baby to go with her designer life?'

Justina flinched. Did he really believe her capable

of doing such a cold-blooded thing? 'That's the most absurd thing I've ever heard.'

'And what better candidate for her baby's father than me?' he continued, as if she hadn't spoken.

'*You?*'

'Yes, me.' Automatically he pulled his powerful shoulders back as his proud words hissed into the air. 'Strong and virile. The alpha of the pack. Women are programmed to want a man like me to father their child. That's why they thrust themselves on me at every opportunity.'

For a moment she was tempted to point out that he had been the one doing the thrusting, but she recognised that this was no time to attempt humour. Not when he was essentially accusing her of having used him as some sort of unknowing *sperm donor*.

'I'm not continuing with this ridiculous discussion any longer,' she said. 'Go and mull over your crazy conspiracy theories somewhere else. I'm tired and I need to pack. I have a plane to catch.'

He watched as she rubbed two fingers tiredly across her forehead. 'You're going home?'

'Yes, Dante—I'm going home. I'm only just within the legal requirement for flying, if you must know.'

'Why the hell *are* you flying? Why aren't you doing what most women would do in your position—lying on a sofa with your feet up instead of trekking halfway across the globe?'

'I've been working.'

'Of course. I should have guessed.'

'I know that for you it's a dirty word when it comes from a woman's lips—but that's just the way it is. I was working—and now I need to pack. So if you wouldn't mind leaving me to get on with it, I'd appreciate it.'

'As it happens, I would. I'd mind very much.' For the first time he saw the faint shadows which darkened her eyes. 'I presume you're booked on to a scheduled flight?'

'I wasn't planning on flapping my arms and flying to England, if that's what you mean.'

He let out a low breath of irritation. 'That is a completely unsatisfactory state of affairs. You will travel with me instead. On the D'Arezzo jet.'

For a moment she hesitated. 'You've got your own plane now?'

'Yes, I've got my own plane,' he snapped. 'I told you at the wedding that the company was doing well—you didn't bother to ask *how* well. But I don't know why that should come as a surprise, when *my* career never made you sit up and take notice. It was always about *you*—wasn't it, Justina?'

He said it in a way which filled Justina with rebellion. Already he was trying to take over. To use his power and his wealth to control her movements. Earlier in the day she'd been feeling lonely—but now she could see that there were worse things than having to deal with an unplanned pregnancy on her own. Like having Dante call the shots and expect her to fall in with his wishes.

'I will not travel on your plane,' she said quietly. 'I already have my ticket and I'm intending to use it. Before you ask, I will be travelling in first class and I will be perfectly comfortable. I don't need your money and what it can buy. That's why I've always made my own. Why I've always been so protective of my career and my independence. Don't you realise that I'm not impressed by your wealth, Dante? I never was.'

There was a pause while their eyes clashed in a silent battle of wills. Yes, he thought bitterly, she had always made it perfectly clear that she didn't need *him*.

'But I'm not trying to impress you,' he said quietly. 'On the contrary, I am merely trying to make you see sense. Because this is no longer just about you and what makes *you* happy—although God knows that's been your main consideration for so long that it's difficult to see how you could ever change your behaviour. You seem to forget that you carry my child within you, and I have a responsibility towards that unborn life.'

She felt her heart contract. 'But you don't—'

'Now, we can do this one of two ways.' His unequivocal words cut through her protest. 'You can force me to carry you kicking and screaming through the foyer of this beautiful hotel—with all the attendant embarrassment and publicity that will cause. Publicity which will be abhorrent to me and to the D'Arezzo corporation. But if I have to do it, then I will. Be under no illusion about that.' There was a pause as his dark gaze scorched through her. 'Or we can do this the easy way. You can go and do your packing and let me fly you back to England and all you have to do is sit back and let it happen. Which is far better for you—and for the baby. Surely even you can see that?'

Justina pursed her lips together, afraid that she was going to do something stupid—like bursting into noisy tears of frustration. He still thought he could march right in and take over her life. Even worse, he didn't just think it—he was actually going ahead and *doing* it, in that powerful and pig-headed way of his. He had her backed into a corner and she knew it—just as she knew that his forceful words were underpinned with truth. It *was* better for the baby, and this *was* no longer just about her.

And if she was being brutally honest hadn't his words produced a flicker of comfort somewhere deep inside her? A feeling which was distracting, because comfort had been absent from her life for so long. For months now she'd carried on travelling and working as she'd done all her life while her belly had got bigger and bigger. She'd tried to convince herself that she was a perfect example of an independent woman who could do this on her own. But lately it had felt lonely, and sometimes in the middle of the night it had even felt scary.

At this precise moment she felt tired—and Dante was standing in front of her like a symbol of everything which was strong and vital. But it was *dangerous* to buy into that. Everything that he did came with some sort of clause. He never offered something without demanding a whole lot back in return. She should remember that.

'It seems that you've got your own way as usual,' she said.

Dante gave a bitter laugh as she spoke the sulky little phrase without any apparent sense of irony. Didn't she realise that she was the one person who had *stopped* him getting his own way and thus had marred his personal track record of success? That she was the one and only person who had ever defied him?

'Maybe you should hold on to that thought, Justina,' he said. 'It might save you from useless rebellion in the future.'

CHAPTER SIX

'THIS IS WHERE you live?'

Justina fought against an inescapable feeling of weariness as Dante stood like a dark avenger in the centre of her apartment and bit out his critical question. Despite the undeniable luxury of his private jet she was exhausted after the long flight, and the traffic from the airport to her East London home had been horrendous. And now she was being forced to stomach the sight of Dante dominating her private space, which was making her feel edgier still. She wished he would just go away and leave her alone—and yet she knew him well enough to realise that he wasn't going anywhere.

Because nothing between them had been settled.

No decisions had been made about the baby during that flight from Singapore. He had settled down to tackle a huge pile of work and largely ignored her. At the time she had been grateful for the respite—relieved not to have to tackle a difficult subject beneath the eyes of the gorgeous stewardesses who worked on his plane. She'd even pulled her notebook from her bag in a retaliatory gesture, but she'd been far too het-up to be able to concentrate on her latest song.

She had tried to buffer herself against the curious volatility of her emotions during that long journey, and yet it had proved almost impossible to remain calm and immune to him. She despaired of the ever-present desire she experienced whenever he was near—as if her body had been hard-wired to make her want him even when she was this pregnant. She didn't know how to make it go away. And now she was beginning to realise that they couldn't keep putting off the inevitable talk about the future.

'Yes, it's where I live,' she said, putting a pile of unopened mail down on the table. 'What's the matter with it?'

Dante glanced around, not bothering to hide his disapproval. It was a vast open-plan apartment which was perfect for a career woman, but not for a baby. There were too many sharp corners, too many glass surfaces—and the furniture was coloured an impractical shade of oatmeal. He'd been to many sophisticated apartments like this but they always left him cold. In Tuscany he had a *palazzo* which was centuries old, and in New York his home was a faded brownstone filled with antiques. He didn't *do* modern—and wasn't that yet another great difference between him and this woman? She had no great love for the past. She'd once told him that was because her own history was so full of gaps—and yet *his* history was what defined him.

Walking over to the window, he stared out at the stately dome of St Paul's Cathedral and the glittering skyscrapers beyond, before turning round to face her.

'This is no place for a baby,' he said.

There had been several times recently when Justina might have been inclined to agree with him, but hearing Dante say it was different from thinking it herself. 'Don't tell me—a baby can't be happy unless it's living in some cute little house with roses growing around the door?' she said sarcastically. 'Or, as in your case, some whacking great *palazzo* nestling in the Tuscan hills?'

'Don't be naïve, Justina. How many other women in this block have babies?'

She frowned. 'What's that got to do with it?'

'So already we're talking social isolation.'

'For a *newborn*?'

'For you, too!' he snapped. 'New mothers need people around them for all kinds of reasons. And what about that tiny elevator?'

'What about it?'

'How the hell are you planning to get a buggy in there?' He looked around again, only this time he appeared to be seeking out something in particular. His dark gaze finally settled on her. 'Where *is* the buggy?'

'Buggy?'

His voice was dangerously quiet, and he appeared to be choosing his words with care. 'Please tell me you've bought our child something in which to transport it. Just like you've bought a cot and clothes and all the other things he or she will require. Do you have all those very necessary things, Justina—and, if so, would you mind telling me where they are?'

Still reeling from that wholly possessive 'our child', which had flowed so fluidly from his lips, she met his eyes, unprepared for the wave of guilt which washed over her. 'No,' she said, and her voice was little more than a whisper. 'I haven't bought a thing. Not yet.'

For a long moment there was silence, before Dante slowly took in her words. 'Not yet' she had said, while looking so ripe with child that he wouldn't have been shocked if she'd suddenly gone into labour right there on the oatmeal sofa. No, that wasn't quite true—he *would* be pretty shocked if that happened.

'Why not?' he demanded. 'What are you waiting for?'

His words were like bullets, and Justina felt as if she'd just removed the vest which might have bounced them back at him. All the fight went out of her—because how could she possibly explain that her life had been non-stop activity for the past thirty-five weeks? That she'd been afraid to turn down any work since she'd first stared aghast at the telltale blue line which had confirmed her pregnancy? That she hadn't wanted people to think she was going to retire or start taking things easy because she still needed to work—baby or no baby? She was going to have to work for all kinds of reasons—the main one being her own sense of crippling insecurity, which always lurked just below the surface of her life.

Hadn't it been easier to cram her life full of jobs? Much easier to have things which kept her busy rather than to have to think about a future she'd never envisaged and which she still couldn't quite imagine. But as she met Dante's gaze she could see that her actions might easily be interpreted as selfishness. And hadn't that always been one of his number one accusations against her? That she was one of a terrible breed of women who refused to put other people first—or rather put their man first?

'I kept putting it off,' she said. 'Maybe it was an extended form of denial that it's actually happening. I've been to all the childbirth classes....' Her voice tailed off as she remembered the ignominy of *that*. Everyone else had been part of a gleeful couple—each man proudly patting his partner's bump at every opportunity and religiously doing all the breathing exercises. One man had even given up soft cheese and alcohol in order to 'share his wife's experience'. Justina had just felt such an *oddity* in their midst. Maybe they'd found it slightly embarrassing that she didn't have a partner—that she'd clammed up whenever they had tried to quiz her about her baby's father. And hadn't she felt so unbelievably *lonely* as she'd tried to stem her envy of their seemingly uncomplicated and ordinary lives?

'It just seemed so unreal,' she continued slowly. 'Like

it wasn't really happening to me. As if I'd wake up one morning and find that it had all been a mistake.'

His gaze was still fixed on her and she waited for some control freak tirade to follow because she'd dared to neglect the material requirements of the D'Arezzo heir. But to her surprise there was no outburst. Just that same faintly despairing expression in his dark eyes, which was infinitely worse. She thought that he'd never seemed more distant as he stood there, his powerful body seeming to absorb all the light in her usually airy apartment. But there was something compelling about him which drew the eye so that it became impossible to look anywhere else other than at him.

'What do you do to relax?' he asked suddenly.

The question was so unexpected that she didn't have time to concoct a convincing answer. Instead, she shrugged. 'I'm not very good at relaxing.'

'I can tell. You look worn out,' he said softly. 'So why don't you think about the baby for once—instead of your unquenchable desire to be number one in the music business? Go and take a bath, or something. Isn't that what women usually do to relax?'

'You would know about that better than I do, Dante.' She was about to add that she would have a bath when *she* wanted one—and preferably after he'd gone—but his phone had started ringing and he'd clicked to answer it. And unbelievably, he was holding up a forefinger to silence her while he listened.

She contemplated telling him to go and take his calls

somewhere else—but she was damned if she was going to stand there like some sort of simpering secretary, waiting patiently for him to finish his conversation. Instead, she stomped into the bathroom and locked the door behind her, turning the taps full on and recklessly dolloping in far too much lime and mandarin bath foam, before she hit the music button and then lowered herself into the foamy water.

When she'd first moved into this apartment she'd had a sophisticated sound system installed which played music in all the rooms. Usually she pressed the 'shuffle' button, so that she never knew which track was coming next. But today she selected *Metamorphosis*—which had been one of the Lollipops' most successful albums. A success which had come at a cost.

It was the album she'd been writing when her relationship with Dante was breaking up. She hadn't been able to listen to it for years but her reasons for needing to hear it now were important. No, they were vital. She needed to revisit that dark place she'd been in. She needed to remember the heartbreak and the desperation she'd felt as it had all slipped away from her. To remind herself that the occasional twinge of isolation was nothing to the pain she'd suffered in the past.

She lay back in the warm water, the shiny mound of her belly emerging from the white suds as the sound of the music filled the bathroom.

It hurt. It hurt more than she had expected it to. The lyrics of one song in particular felt like having a bucket of salt poured over an open wound, and she flinched as the memories all came flooding back. It was a song which had soared up the charts. Women had bought it in droves. She'd even been approached about having it used in the film score of a romantic comedy, but she had said no—even though her agent had hit the roof when she'd told him. She hadn't been able to bear the thought of having it associated with comedy when it symbolised the bleakest time of her life. In fact, she'd always regretted releasing it as a single. It had been played on the radio so much that for a while she'd stopped listening in order to preserve her sanity.

She'd written it when she'd got back from finding Dante in bed with that blonde, pouring all her feelings out into a song because she hadn't been able to bear the shame of telling anyone else what had happened. She'd entitled the track 'Her' and the words were still unbearably painful to hear.

> *Does she know the things you said*
> *When you were lying in my bed?*
> *Your words of love became a slur*
> *When you whispered them to her.*

Justina wanted to scream. To turn the music off and with it the images it brought back—but she couldn't move. She was marooned in a great tub of bath water, feeling and looking like a beached whale, her usual agility long gone. So she closed her eyes and waited for the track to finish.

The water was almost cold by the time she carefully got out, hoping that Dante would have taken the hint and gone.

But he hadn't gone. He was still talking on the phone, looking out of the window as he conversed in his native tongue. He must have heard her enter the room—even though she was moving soundlessly on bare feet—for he turned round, his eyes narrowing when he saw her.

Maybe she should have put on some jeans and a sweater, not the full-length silken robe which she'd wrapped tightly over her baby bump. But why *should* she start turning her whole life around to fit in with him? She was dressed for bed and she intended to go to bed—perhaps he might take the hint and leave her to it.

His voice slowed as he watched her push a lock of damp hair back behind her ear, and he said something in Italian before cutting the connection and sliding the phone back into his jacket pocket.

'I thought you'd have gone by now,' she said ungraciously as she slumped down onto the sofa.

'I was listening to the music. Unsurprisingly, the acoustics in your apartment are the best I've ever heard.' His smile was brief, but damning. 'Tell me, do you always listen to your own songs when you're lying in the bath?'

If she said *'never'*, wouldn't that indicate that he could still unsettle her enough to make her behave in an uncharacteristic way? *And she didn't have to justify herself to him.*

'That's none of your business. I can listen to what I like. Frankly, I'm surprised you're still here—not least because that last song must have made you feel intensely uncomfortable. Or maybe not.' Her eyes challenged him with a bravado she was far from feeling. 'Maybe it feeds your massive ego to hear yourself written about in a song.'

'Not that particular song, no,' he reflected. 'It was unforgivable for you to take our private disagreement and throw it into the public arena.'

'Perhaps if you hadn't behaved like a total sleaze then I might have found something good to write about you.'

'"A total sleaze"?'

His eyes narrowed, but she could tell by the way that he was tapping his forefinger against his lips that he was furious.

'Is that what you think I am, Justina?'

He was walking towards her now, with a look on his face which was making her shiver. Actually, it was making her do much more than shiver. It was making the soft, curling excitement at the pit of her belly slowly begin to unfurl. She knew she ought to move, to run away—but her slumped position on the sofa meant that she wasn't able to run anywhere. *And deep down she knew she didn't want to.*

'It doesn't matter what I think you are,' she said.

'No?'

'No. You're nothing to me any more, Dante.'

For a moment their gazes locked, and Justina held her breath as he walked round the back of the sofa to stand behind her, so that she couldn't see him. She could feel a strange kind of tension begin to shimmer in the air around them.

'I think it does matter.' There was a pause as he brushed a fingertip over the back of her neck. 'You don't like me very much, do you?'

She shook her head. 'No.'

'Brutal, but honest,' he mused, his fingertip retracing the path it had just taken, as if he was fascinated by the innocuous column of flesh he found there.

She tried to fight against the sudden whisper of pleasure that touch had given her. 'What are you doing?'

He began to massage her shoulders, briefly expelling a breath as he felt her soft flesh beneath his fingers again. 'I'm trying to make you relax, but it isn't easy because you are very tense, *tesoro*,' he observed softly. 'Very, very tense.'

Justina swallowed. She ought to assert herself. She ought to tell him to stop. But how could she bear to do that when it felt this good? His fingers were kneading at the tightness in her shoulders and she could feel the tight knots dissolving as if by magic. His thumbs began to circle rhythmically at the base of her neck and it was impossible not to just go with it. She told herself that the caress of his fingers on her skin was dangerous. She knew that. But it had been so long since she had been touched. Not since that night back in Norfolk, when their baby had been conceived.

She closed her eyes. 'Dante—'

'Shh.' His fingers continued with their steady movement. 'Don't talk.'

'You shouldn't be doing that.'

'All I'm doing is making you relax.'

But that wasn't all he was doing. He must know that. Because the tension which had melted away had now been replaced by a very different kind. She could feel it building in the air around them—like the heavy electricity you got before a violent thunderstorm. She could feel the melting ache of heat between her thighs and the insistent tingling of her breasts as she yearned for him to touch them. And wasn't it appalling that the woman who was due to give birth in a few short weeks should be feeling this rising tide of need?

So stop him!

Her throat felt dry, her mouth so parched that she could barely get the words out. 'I don't think—'

'Good. Don't think. Just feel.'

And—oh, God—it was all too easy to do that. Sinfully easy. His hands were working deeper into the flesh around her shoulders and he had drifted two thumbs down over her ribcage. Her heart was fluttering wildly in response. Surely she was mistaken but had he…had he just brushed his hands over her breasts? Yes. There it was again. Definitely. The whisper of his fingertips was butterfly-light but achingly accurate.

'Dante—'

'For once in your life, will you just shut up?' he questioned, splaying his hand over one peaking nipple and letting his thumb circle over the tight bud.

She began to squirm with excitement. She couldn't help it. She wanted to call his name out loud. She wanted him to walk round to the front of the sofa, to pull her into his arms and start kissing her and make love to her properly. But he wasn't doing that. He was… He was…

She gasped as he leaned over her, so that his lips were on the top of her head. She could hear the heavy sound of his own breathing and it was echoing the sound of her own. She could smell the sandalwood scent of his aftershave and feel the warmth of his flesh as he touched her. His hand had skated down over the swollen mound of her belly and he was pushing aside the folds of her silken robe. She could feel her thighs parting—as if she was a puppet and someone was pulling her strings. Well, *he* was. That was exactly what he was doing. He was skating little circles over the cool skin of her inner thighs until she was gasping helplessly with pleasure. And then his finger flicked over her moist and eager flesh until it alighted on the tight little nub and she opened her thighs wider. She gave another gasp as he began to make that achingly familiar movement, her hunger briefly tempered by the fear that he might stop.

But he didn't stop. He carried on with what he was doing. Stroking his finger against her aroused flesh until she was past caring about anything—victim to her own urgent needs as she called out his name like a betrayal.

It happened in a rush. One minute she was climbing towards the blissful summit, still shadowed by the fear that the peak might elude her, or that it might not happen at all. But Dante always delivered. Every time. Only never like this. Never quite like this. She found herself making little cries that sounded like pleas as she spasmed helplessly around his finger.

Time shifted and slowed as she drifted back down from a dazed state of bliss, unsure what to do next even if her weighted limbs had been capable of any kind of movement. All she knew was that he was tugging her robe back into place before dropping a light kiss on top of her head almost as an afterthought.

He walked around the sofa and stood facing her with an expression on his face which she couldn't fathom, even if she'd had the energy to try. She could feel the colour still flooding her cheeks, and the intense dryness in her mouth which made the thought of speaking seem like a chore. Her head felt as heavy as lead but she forced herself to keep her chin lifted, because she wasn't going to cower away and pretend that nothing had happened.

'What…what did you do that for?'

He gave a short laugh. 'You're now going to tell me you loathed every minute of it, I suppose?'

She wished that the telltale heat in her cheeks would

magically disappear. 'That's…' And why was her voice sounding so infuriatingly *husky*? 'That's not the point.'

'I thought it was exactly the point.' He shrugged his shoulders in a particularly Italian way and his lips curved into a smile of undeniable satisfaction. 'You were uptight, so I started to massage your shoulders. And then you seemed a little…*turned on*…so I did exactly what you wanted me to do.'

For a moment she looked at him in disbelief, but the unrepentant expression on his face was nearly as damning as his words. 'You hateful…*bastard*!'

'Guilty as charged.' His eyes narrowed. 'But while you might hate me, Justina, I hope you won't be hypocritical enough to deny that you still want me. You made that pretty clear.'

Just as he wanted her. Her face was flushed and belligerent and she was glaring at him, and he was tempted—oh, how he was tempted. Would it be the end of the world if he joined her on that great big sofa and started to kiss her? He could feel the throb of desire at his groin and imagined the sweetness of her fingers stroking him there. Imagined her guiding him into her sticky warmth. He found himself wondering what position he would have to take to make it more comfortable for her, because he had never made love to a pregnant woman before.

He shifted his weight as desire fought a fierce battle with reason. She was *pregnant*, he reminded himself, and she was pregnant with *his child*. Maybe he shouldn't have touched her like that—but hadn't the restless wriggle of her curiously sensual body made it impossible to do otherwise?

Averting his gaze from the anger which was still sparking from her eyes, he glanced at his watch. 'And, much as I hate to miss out on today's dose of character assassination, I really must go. My plane will have been refuelled and I'm flying back to the States.'

Justina hugged the lapels of her robe closer. 'That's the best bit of news I've had all day.'

'I'm sure it is. But don't worry, because I'll be back in time for the birth.'

'You don't have to.'

'Oh, but I do. You may not need me, Justina—but my baby does.' He pulled a business card from his wallet and put it down on the table next to her handbag. 'You'll find all my details there, including my private number.'

'Gosh, I *am* privileged. Or maybe not. How many women are in possession of one of these, I wonder?'

'You'll also find the number of my assistant, who has been instructed to help you,' he continued smoothly, as if her interruption had been nothing but a minor irritation. 'Anything you want, you ring Tiffany—she's very efficient. If you can't face furnishing the nursery yourself—as seems to be the case—then she can do it all from New York.'

Justina's post-orgasmic lethargy was replaced by a growing feeling of rage. Tiffany? Who the hell was Tiffany? He wanted his *assistant* to go out and buy stuff for *her* baby, did he? While managing to make *her* sound useless and helpless in the process?

With an effort she stopped slumping against the cushions and sat up to glare at him. 'And what else does *Tiffany* do?' she questioned. 'Is it part of her job description to provide extras for the boss?'

'I try never to mix business with pleasure,' he answered coolly. 'And you really shouldn't be getting yourself worked up like that. You've already had enough excitement for one afternoon, so why don't you go and get some rest?'

'Oh, just go,' she said, shutting her eyes to block out the sight of his undeniably gorgeous face. She kept them closed until she'd heard the front door click behind him, and when she opened them again he was gone.

She sighed. If only it was as easy to get rid of the memory of what she'd just let him do to her.

CHAPTER SEVEN

'DANTE WANTS TO KNOW whether you've received the brochure, Miss Perry?'

Justina's fingers tightened around the telephone receiver as she listened to the transatlantic accent of Tiffany Jones and wondered why the hell she hadn't just let this call go through to her answering service. She was feeling lumpy and lethargic enough without having to endure yet another of these polite and all-too-frequent queries which had been coming from Dante's personal assistant in his New York office.

But it would be demeaning to give in to what she really wanted to say, which was: *Are you sleeping with the father of my baby?* Surely a situation like this demanded that she act with an unflappability equal to that of the cool-sounding Tiffany.

'Yes, thank you. I've received it,' said Justina, recalling the ritzy attachment which had pinged through on to her computer last week, offering a cornucopia of luxurious items for the more privileged baby.

'And did you like it?' Tiffany's voice was eager.

'Would you like us to go ahead and order the crib for you—and the stroller?'

Us? *Us?* Justina's hand wrapped itself around the receiver as if it was Dante's neck she was squeezing. Resisting the urge to tell the woman that in England they were called a cot and a buggy, she walked into the smaller of her two bedrooms to see one of each standing there, all new and shiny-bright. The primrose-yellow walls of the nursery been adorned with a giant jungle scene, and a mobile of tigers and lions swirled down from the ceiling, adding to the storybook feel of the room. A smile of satisfaction curved her lips. From all the fuss that Tiffany had been making from New York you'd have thought that decorating and furnishing a nursery was right up there with brain surgery.

'Can you please tell Dante that none of that will be necessary?' she said crisply.

'I can tell him,' said Tiffany doubtfully. 'But I think he'd prefer to speak to you himself, Miss Perry.'

Well, why didn't he pick up the phone himself, instead of asking his wretched assistant to make the call? 'I'm afraid that I don't really have the time—'

'Justina?'

Dante's velvet-edged drawl came on to the line and Justina could have screamed. Why weren't any of them listening to what she was saying?

'What do you want?' she questioned ungraciously.

'I want to know how you're feeling today.'

'Honestly? I'm tired, and I'm feeling like a whale,

and I'm fed up with these regular interrogations of yours—'

'And have you given any more thought to my question?' he interrupted smoothly.

'I've given it a good deal of thought and my feelings haven't changed.' She sucked in a deep and determined breath. 'I don't want anyone there with me at the birth—especially you. It isn't mandatory to have a birthing partner, you know.'

She could hear what sounded like Dante tapping his finger against the phone. 'I know it isn't mandatory,' he said. 'But it's certainly preferable. You can't do it all on your own, Justina.'

'On the contrary, I can—and what's more, I intend to.' She paused for a moment as her abdomen tensed with a sharp and disturbing kind of twinge. 'I don't need anyone while I go through what is a perfectly natural procedure. And it isn't as if we're in some kind of *relationship*, is it?' Her mind took her back to the last time she'd seen him, when a seemingly innocent massage of her shoulders had turned into a sensual act which still made her cheeks burn with embarrassment whenever she thought about it. No wonder he thought she was some kind of puppet when she'd behaved like that. *So show him you're not some kind of puppet.* 'I'm an independent woman, Dante. Just in case you'd forgotten.'

'How could I possibly forget,' he questioned acidly, 'when you never fail to remind me?'

'Then why don't you try listening to me for a change

instead of forcing your will on me? I could—' But the rest of the sentence froze in her throat as an iron-hot band of pain clamped itself around her belly.

'Justina? Are you still there?'

The intensity of the pain was so unexpected and so powerful that she clapped her hand over the phone so that he wouldn't be able to hear her panting her way through it. It wasn't until it had passed that she spoke again, in a voice which was unnaturally bright. 'Sorry about that—I thought I heard someone at the door.'

She could hear the frown in his voice. 'Are you okay?'

'I'm *fine.*'

'When you did you last see the doctor?'

'When I was supposed to see him—last week. I have all my appointments written down neatly in my diary and I have been following them to the letter. Now, will you stop fussing?' she said. 'I'm perfectly capable of having a baby without having you checking up on me every five minutes like some kind of demented midwife. And I really have to go—I'm in the middle of writing a song and I must get the words down before they go out of my head. Don't worry, Dante. I'll let you know the minute something happens.'

She cut him off without another word and walked over to the window, trying to shake off her strange feeling of restlessness and the power he always had to unsettle her. She didn't need to feel any more unsettled than she currently did and it couldn't be good for her *or* the baby. She felt as if the air was pressing down on her, and the rain which had been falling for seven days straight showed no sign of stopping. She'd been stuck inside all day, and yet the last thing she wanted was to go outside and brave the elements.

She should watch a film—or read that book she'd bought, which everyone was raving on about—the one whose hero seemed to have modelled himself on the Marquis de Sade. She knew that relaxation was vital during these late stages of her pregnancy, but her strong work ethic meant that she always felt guilty if she did nothing.

She flicked through the TV channels and found a woman yelling at a weasely man who really needed to do something about his skin. The woman's inarticulate insults were at first amusing—and then a touch disturbing. Because Justina realised that what motivated them was frustration that the man wouldn't do what the woman wanted him to do—which was to love her.

I'm never going to be that woman, Justina vowed fiercely as another sharp band of pain tightened across her abdomen. *I'm never going to have hopeless expectations of a man who can never meet them, because that's a sure-fire recipe for unhappiness.* Much better to be independent and free of emotional pain.

But then another very physical pain caught her by surprise. It was so strong that she had to stand perfectly still and cling to the back of the sofa. It wasn't until they started coming regularly that she realised she was in labour.

She tried to stay calm and remember what to do. *Stay at home for as long as possible. Time the contractions and call the hospital.* Another wave clamped like a burning iron around her middle, and she was gasping a little as she picked up the phone and spoke to a midwife.

'Come in now,' said the midwife. 'Have you got someone with you?'

'I'm on my way,' said Justina, neatly avoiding the question.

But they asked her again when she'd been checked in to the birthing suite as she lay on the bed, having her blood pressure monitored.

'Is the father on his way, Miss Perry?'

'No.' Justina shook her head. 'He's in New York.'

'Does he know that you're in labour?'

She thought about Dante seeing her like this. She thought about how nothing but a capricious fate had brought them together. Hadn't she told him that she was independent and that she didn't actually *need* him? Well, that hadn't just been bluster—she'd *meant* it.

She shook her head. 'No, he doesn't know.'

'Someone here could easily—'

'I don't want him here,' declared Justina.

Did she imagine the look of disapproval which passed between the midwife and her student? But then another pain came, and it was so powerful that it obliterated everything, and she stopped wondering if she was being judged for her morals or her cold-heartedness.

Time slowed and she felt disorientated—only the relentless contractions brought reality into sharp and clear focus. Hours passed by in a blur of pain as Justina tried to remember all the things she'd learned at her antenatal classes and put them into practice. She paced the floor. She crouched down on her hands and knees as sweat poured from her brow. She tried not to gasp, but not gasping became impossible when the midwife examined her and announced that she'd gone into 'second stage'.

'I don't care what stage I'm in! I just want this bloody baby out!' shouted Justina recklessly.

She heard the sound of some commotion at the door, where the student midwife stood talking to someone. She heard an unmistakable Italian accent speaking low words edged with fierce intent.

'Just ask her. Please.'

The student came over to the bed, her cheeks looking flushed. 'There's a man outside who says he's the father of your baby and he wants to come in. He says his name is Dante D'Arezzo and please could I ask you.'

In a brief respite between contractions it occurred to Justina that this was possibly the first time in Dante's life that he'd had to ask for anything without being guaranteed the desired response. But her reasons for wanting to exclude him seemed *petty* in the light of what was happening. Justina looked towards the door and there he stood—six feet plus of dark and brooding determination. And *strength*, she realized as she registered the tension in his powerful shoulders. Couldn't she use a little of that strength right now?

'Let him in,' she croaked, and he must have heard her because in an instant he was at her bedside, his expression impenetrable as he looked down at her. But the words of recrimination she'd expected were absent as he brushed aside a lock of matted hair with a hand which was remarkably gentle.

'I'm here now,' he said simply.

'Is that supposed to make me feel better?'

'I'm rather hoping it might.'

For some reason his words made her feel bad. 'Dante, I didn't want to—'

'Shh. I doesn't matter. I'm here,' he repeated. 'And that's all that matters.'

She swallowed. 'It...*hurts*.'

'Then hold on to me. Go on, hold on—as tight as you like. Hurt *me* instead, if it makes you feel better.'

She told herself that it was stupid to want to cling to him. To hold him so tightly so that he would never let her go. But all her inhibitions seemed to be melting away as the demands of her body took over and she clutched him like a drowning woman snatching at a floating branch.

'I'm hot,' she added.

'Then lose the gown.' The corners of his lips curved. 'It's not the best thing I've ever seen you in.'

She almost smiled back as he helped her tug the sweat-soaked hospital issue garment from her body and the coolness of the air washed over her naked skin. But then came another of those contractions, and when she had breath enough to speak she shuddered out the fear which was threatening to overwhelm her.

'I'm so scared that something's going to go wrong.'

His black gaze caught hold of her and enveloped her. He lifted up the hand which wasn't digging into his and briefly touched it to his lips. 'The chances of that happening are infinitesimally small. You're in the best possible hands. You know that, Jus. You've told me often enough. How did you put it? A perfectly natural procedure that women have been going through since the beginning of time.'

Had she really said that? Had she really sounded so stupidly confident when now she felt as nervous as a child on the first day of school?

Her fingernails dug even farther into his hand. *'I want to push!'*

Dante flicked a glance at the midwife, who nodded. 'Then push, *tesoro*,' he urged softly. 'Go ahead and push all you like.'

'Arrgh!'

Her anguished cry made him feel helpless—Dante felt more powerless than he'd ever felt in his life. Frustration washed over him as he watched her writhe, but he did what little he could to help her. He smoothed away her hair when she thrashed her head wildly against the pillow, and dabbed cool water at her temples which briefly made her moan with gratitude. But only briefly.

All too soon the tension in the room increased, along with the rising sound of her cries. Dante watched as the movements of the midwives became brisker, though one of them paused long enough to raise her head and ask, 'Do you want to come and see your baby being born, Signor D'Arezzo?'

Dante met Justina's eyes and wordlessly she nodded. For one minute he thought she might be about to make some smart comment, and perhaps if she hadn't been in the middle of giving birth she might have done, but she closed her eyes again and screwed up her face with a fierce concentration.

And then it all became very urgent. The air pulsed with taut words and fractured cries as Justina gave an almighty push. His breath caught in his throat as he saw a dark slick of hair appear, followed by the seemingly impossible appearance of a bruised and bloodied baby as she pushed again. And his heart clenched as the infant opened its mouth and howled and somebody said, "It's a boy!"

They put the slippery infant into the cradle of his hands as they cut the cord, and Dante's throat was so tight he could barely breathe. His baby. His son. So tiny and so helpless. He could feel the tears pricking at his eyes as the midwife took the baby from him. She cleaned him, before placing him onto Justina's breast, where he began to suckle, his eyes fixed on his mother's as if they'd known each other for a very long time. Silently, Dante watched as Justina touched a finger to the newborn's smooth cheek and gave a secretive kind of smile.

And in that moment he had never wanted her quite so much.

CHAPTER EIGHT

JUSTINA WATCHED AS Dante's fingers moved with remarkable dexterity over the tiny baby, his dark head bent as he focussed intently on the task at hand. He was so *careful*, she thought, as if Nico was made of porcelain rather than of flesh and blood. But every so often the intense concentration on his features would soften a little, and he would smile and murmur something in Italian. With an unwanted rush of emotion she acknowledged how tender he could be—and how gentle—and something dangerously close to nostalgia flickered over her.

Forcing her thoughts away from the wistful and back to the purely practical, she looked at the ebony gleam of Dante's head. 'I never thought I'd see you change a nappy,' she observed.

Dante gave Nico a final kiss on his little belly, before raising his head to look at Justina, who sat with an expression of serene interest on her face as she watched him. It was hard to get his head around the fact that she'd given birth less than a month ago, for although she was definitely curvier than she'd used to be she was still as slim as a reed. She looked more casual than he'd ever seen her, with her hair caught into a single plait which fell over one shoulder and a face completely free of make-up. Yet he didn't think he'd ever seen a woman looking as delectable as she did right now. Her skin was soft and clear and her eyes were bright. He found himself wondering whether this was another of wily Mother Nature's safety mechanisms—that a man should feel such overwhelming lust towards the woman who had just borne his child.

'Changing a nappy isn't difficult,' he said as he lifted the drowsy Nico from the changing mat and placed him carefully in his cot.

'Obviously not,' answered Justina, wishing that he'd stop being quite so...*reasonable.* Because this was Dante, she reminded herself. Powerful Dante, who didn't say or do anything without an ulterior motive. She raised her eyebrows in ironic query. 'But I thought that a macho man like you...'

Her words tailed off and he gave a wry smile. 'You make me sound like someone who bares his chest and wears a medallion. There's nothing in the rule book to say that the most masculine of men can't be hands-on with his own baby.' He gave a shrug. 'Although obviously things were very different in my father's day. I'm sure he never changed a nappy in his life.'

Justina started to fold one of Nico's tiny vests as Dante's words forced her to confront something which up until now they'd managed to avoid. 'You haven't really mentioned how your family have reacted to the news. I assume you've told them?'

'Of course. I rang them the night he was born.' She saw his ebony eyes soften with memory. 'My mother is over the moon. This is her first grandchild and she's eager to meet him. All my family are.'

Justina nodded. Of course they were—and she knew they had every right to be. Just as she knew that she couldn't keep putting off the inevitable meeting. She felt as if she'd been living in a bubble since Nico's birth—a feeling which had only been strengthened by Dante's unexpected help with the baby. Had he been worried that she'd be unable to cope or that she'd sink into a mire of postnatal depression? Was that why he'd seamlessly relocated from New York and booked in at the nearby Vinoly Hotel, so that it was easy for him to drop by and visit his son?

She had returned home from the hospital to a delivery of the most beautiful flowers. Gardenias and roses and stephanotis and lily of the valley had been massed into a bouquet so enormous that she'd hardly been able to get it through the front door. The fragrance had been intoxicating, and the brief accompanying note of thanks had made her want to cry. But crying was the last thing she could afford to do. The last thing she ever did. Crying made you weak, and never had she needed her strength as much as she needed it right now.

She remembered turning on Dante as if he'd sent her an explosive device, aware of the sudden tremble of her fingers as they had brushed against the white petals. 'Why did you send me flowers?'

'Isn't it normal for the father to send flowers to the new mother?'

Justina had shaken her head. Of course it was *normal*. But *they* weren't normal, were they? None of this was. A baby had been born to two people who were no longer together. Who didn't even like each other. *And Dante was not a man she could trust.* She should remember that above all else. He might be ladling on sweet words and consideration, but he would be doing it for a reason. And it seemed that one of those reasons had now arrived.

She drew in a deep breath as met his eyes. 'Your mean your mother wants to come and visit?'

He shook his head. 'My mother hates to travel. I was thinking that you and I might take Nico to Tuscany instead. I think it's time he was introduced to his Italian roots.'

She wanted to protest that at four weeks old Nico would barely be conscious of which cot he was in, let alone which country. But Justina knew Dante well enough to realise that her words would fall on deaf ears. He had always been passionate about his homeland, and no amount of reason was ever going to alter that. In fact she was surprised that he had waited this long to bring it up. *That's why he has been so unusually reasonable,* she told herself. The flowers and the nappy-changing and the insistence that she relax in the bath while he looked after Nico—they had all been velvet-coated weapons in his battle to get what he wanted.

But despite the sensation of being manipulated Justina had no intention of refusing his request, no matter how difficult she might find it to return to his family home. Because Nico *needed* family—and her own was never even going to make it past the starting line.

'Do they still hate me?' she questioned, in a voice which didn't actually sound like her voice.

'I think that's an unnecessarily emotive way of putting it, Justina.'

'I thought one of your complaints about me was that I wasn't emotional enough?' That was the main accusation he'd used to hurl at her, usually just before one of her tours, so that they'd always seemed to part with some sort of atmosphere simmering between them. 'I remember you telling me that no woman with a heart could leave her man while she went away on tour.'

Dante met the amber glitter of her eyes. It was true he'd found it unbelievable that she could bear to be away from him for any length of time. He'd thought that her career would pale in comparison to being with the man she professed to love. But apparently not. She had refused to temper her ambition and he had grown impatient with her frequent absences. In the end those absences had chipped away at their relationship, so that many of their snatched reunions had been spent getting to know one another again. Sometimes it had felt as if they were going backwards instead of forward. When it had finally come, his furious ultimatum had seemed inevitable.

'My family didn't hate you,' he said slowly.

There was a pause. 'They didn't make me feel very welcome when I met them.' She could hear that whisper of insecurity in her voice again.

'I think they tried their best.' He reached down into the cot and stroked Nico's head. 'But my mother is an old-fashioned woman who didn't approve of your choice of career—or all the things which came with it.'

'Like mother, like son!' observed Justina wryly, though she recognised that it hadn't just been his mother who had been opposed to her. Dante's brother Luigi had also disapproved—and all the male D'Arezzo cousins had clearly felt the same.

Her mind went back to the welcome party which had been thrown during her first and only visit to the D'Arezzo estate. If only Dante's sister hadn't insisted on playing the Lollipops' latest DVD! Justina remembered the entire family sitting and watching in horror as she'd cavorted across the screen wearing a tiny tutu and a minuscule vest-top. After that they'd treated her as if she was some kind of stripper instead of a legitimate songwriter and performer.

'They didn't think I was the right person for you,' she added. 'I was unsuitable. And of course being English didn't add to my general allure.'

'All Italian mothers want their sons to marry an Italian girl,' he said with a shrug.

'As opposed to an illegitimate nobody whose mother has a track record for breaking up other people's marriages?'

'I think she wondered how our relationship was going to work when you were travelling the world.' There was a pause as his black eyes glittered a question. 'And you must admit that she had a point.'

Justina glanced down at where Nico lay sleeping and tried to imagine Dante ever being this tiny or this helpless. Unsurprisingly, she failed. 'So how did your mother react when you told her who the mother of your baby was?'

Dante hesitated as he considered how best to convey his mother's words. He had expected anger. Rage. A tirade against the Englishwoman who had made those brazen promotional films and flaunted her half-naked body to the world at large. He had thought there would be a dramatic outburst about a woman like *her* returning to the scene and ensnaring her powerful son by becoming pregnant.

But he hadn't bargained for the softening effects of age, nor the primitive desire to see their powerful family line continued. His mother had been widowed for a long time and Dante was her eldest son. It was right that his offspring should be the firstborn, she'd said. The thought of a whole new generation of the D'Arezzo family was enough to sweeten the pill of the mother's identity—and the fact that he wasn't married to her.

*'But you will have to marry her, of course, Dante.
If this baby is a D'Arezzo, then he must be legitimised.'*

Dante remembered his mother's immediate assumption. The way she had smiled the smile of a woman who knew that a hundred candidates would have married her son in an instant. But Dante knew it wasn't as easy as that. Not with Justina. Most women *would* fall over backwards to become a D'Arezzo bride—but not this woman who took such pride in her independence. Who would see no point in marrying for the sake of a baby—especially when their relationship had failed last time around. Yet despite all this, one irrefutable fact remained—*his own fierce familial pride would not countenance his son being illegitimate.*

'Dante?'

He looked up. 'What?'

'I asked how your mother reacted when you told her she was going to be a grandparent.'

'In the same way that any grandparent would react, I guess. With joy and with excitement. I expect your mother was exactly the same?'

Justina twisted the end of her plait with restless fingers. 'You *are* joking?' she said. 'She thinks she's way too young for that particular role.'

'That figures,' he said. But despite her flippant comment, Dante glimpsed the hurt which had briefly clouded Justina's eyes and felt a surge of anger on her behalf. Couldn't her mother have behaved *normally* for once? Couldn't she just have cooed a little and been there for her daughter? 'Did she send anything for Nico?'

Justina laughed. 'A silver napkin ring which he'll probably never use.'

'You know, we'll need to get him a passport as soon as possible,' Dante said suddenly. 'If we're taking him to Tuscany.'

Justina realised that they'd slipped seamlessly from talking about a hypothetical trip to Tuscany to acquiring a passport for the journey—and wasn't that Dante all over? He would always try stealth before he tried coercion but the end result was always the same: he got exactly what he wanted.

Their journey plans were set in motion and Justina went shopping for new clothes, since none of her own seemed right. She wanted to wear something normal and flattering after months of being swaddled in loose clothes, but it was more than that. The last time she'd seen Signora D'Arezzo had been at the height of her fame, when she had very definitely been dressed like a pop star. She'd been into glitter and pizazz and making a statement—but nearly six years down the line her tastes had changed. She still bought trendy, but these days she gravitated towards the less garish.

She loaded up her shopping basket with silk and cashmere and splashed out on some new underwear, telling herself that she was only buying it because her shape had changed. But she felt a flare of colour in her cheeks as her fingers drifted over a lacy thong and she imagined Dante removing it.

Loaded down with baby equipment, they travelled to a private airfield north of London, where the D'Arezzo jet was ready and waiting. They left England on a drizzly day and touched down in Tuscany, where only a few faint clouds floated in an azure sky, and Justina tried to remember the last time she'd had anything approaching a holiday.

At Pisa airport they were whisked straight through the various border controls with the kind of adulation which Justina hadn't witnessed since she'd been on the road with the Lollipops. But then, Dante was on his own territory here, she reminded herself. People knew him. They revered and respected him. The D'Arezzo family had lived in the region for centuries, and his aristocratic air had never been more evident than when people stopped to compliment him on the baby.

Yet she felt wistful as she watched him carry Nico through, while officials beamed and touched the baby's raven curls. And she noticed the sideways looks which greeted her as she followed in his footsteps—the glances at the fingers of her left hand, noticeably bare of a wedding ring or any kind of show of commitment from Dante D'Arezzo.

Perhaps they think I'm the nanny, thought Justina as they walked out to a waiting car. She touched the heavy silk of the jacket she was wearing over black skinny jeans as if to remind herself of who she really was. This was a jacket she'd paid for herself—not gone crawling to a man for an allowance to finance it. She was self-supporting and she should be proud of that.

'You okay?' questioned Dante, looking up from where he'd just finished buckling Nico into a baby car-seat.

'I'm fine,' she said, trying to ignore the butterfly nerves which were building in her stomach.

'You look amazing,' he said softly as the car pulled away.

His statement caught her by surprise and Justina glanced up, slightly appalled to hear herself trotting out that most predictable of responses. 'Do I?'

'You certainly do. Nobody would ever guess you'd had a baby so recently.'

'Until they see the baby, of course,' she said pleasantly, trying to ignore the instinctive sizzle of her skin. She told herself that he was good at making a woman feel as if she was the centre of the universe—heaven only knew he'd had enough practice at it. *He's a player,* she reminded herself, *and all players do that. He went to bed with someone barely a week after your engagement had broken down. That is not the behaviour of a man who professed to love you and only you.*

She thought about all the things which remained unsaid between them. That strange *intimacy* which they'd shared during the birth, when Dante had been there for her in a way she'd never imagined he could. He'd been strong and protective and gentle, and in those highly emotional moments she'd felt close to him again. She had thought she wouldn't want him there, but now she didn't like to imagine what it might have been like if he hadn't been.

But there were other things which also remained unsaid—things she wasn't proud of. Neither of them had mentioned that erotic encounter on the sofa, after which he had just walked out of the door as if nothing very remarkable had happened. And he hadn't made any move on her since, had he? Even now that her body had pinged back into shape and she'd begun to forge her own routine around Nico, Dante still hadn't looked at her with anything approaching desire.

She kept telling herself that having no physical intimacy made sense on every level. It was too easy to build dreams when a man was making love to you… But that didn't stop her wanting him or being so *aware* of him. As if her body had been programmed to react with excitement whenever he was close.

Turning her head, she stared out the window as the car drove past high green mountains and tried to concentrate on the beauty of the Tuscan countryside. All she had to do was be a good mother to her baby—that was the most important thing.

Before long, the motorway gave way to more rural roads, and although it had been over five years since she'd last been here Justina was surprised by how familiar it all seemed. The D'Arezzo home wasn't immediately visible from the road—mainly because the gardens and estate had been planted so that it would blend into the land around it. A long drive led up to the house and behind it soared more green hills, studded with ancient olive trees and a variety of fruit orchards, and lower down were the prize-winning D'Arezzo vines themselves.

The *palazzo* grew closer, with its dark golden walls and its shuttered windows. Justina stared up at its clock tower and all the different wings which had been added over the years and couldn't fail to be impressed—just as she'd been the first time she'd set eyes on it. Here lay centuries of stability and continuity and a definite place in the local community. It was something she'd never had herself, and a lump rose in her throat as she realised that this was not just Dante's heritage but Nico's, too. That his blood made him part of this place and she had no right to deny him that heritage.

The big car came to a halt in the courtyard, and she was surprised to see Dante's mother waiting for them. In the past, the housekeeper had greeted them, and the meeting with Beatrix D'Arezzo had been postponed until the formal pre-dinner drinks.

Justina watched as Dante carried Nico towards his mother and hung back a little as she saw Beatrix lean eagerly towards the baby. Saw her touch his cheek with wondering fingers before exclaiming, '*Caspita, e uguale a suo padre!*'

Justina smiled as Beatrix came forward to greet her. Her crash course in Italian years earlier might have only left her with a rudimentary grasp of the language, but she understood the gist of *that*. Baby Nico *was* certainly the image of his father!

'Justina!' said Signora D'Arezzo with a smile. 'Welcome back. And congratulations on the birth of such a beautiful little boy.'

The words sounded genuine and Justina nodded, acutely aware that Dante was watching her.

'*Mille grazie,* Signora D'Arezzo,' she answered, and then she smiled back. 'He's gorgeous, isn't he?'

'Gorgeous, indeed, and the image of his father at the same age!' said Beatrix indulgently. 'But you look tired, Justina. Travelling is always tiring—especially for such a new mother. Would you like to see your rooms, so that you can all settle in?'

Justina gave a grateful smile. 'That sounds perfect. Thank you.'

'Dante?' Signora D'Arezzo turned to her son and said something in Italian before turning back to Justina. 'We haven't had a baby here for a long time, but we will do our best to make you feel at home.'

It was Beatrix's *kindness* which was affecting her more than anything, Justina realised as she nodded her thanks. Or maybe it was more complex than that—because Signora D'Arezzo was exhibiting a *motherliness* towards her which she wasn't used to. *Her* mother had never been big on hugging—unless it involved a man with a big wallet. She'd treated her daughter more like an adornment than a real person—and hadn't that been one of the things which had made Justina determined to be as hands-on as possible with her own son, determined that he should feel her love from the start?

She followed Dante as he carried the baby through the winding corridors of the ancient villa before stopping before an enormous set of wooden doors. Inside, the main room was tall and arched, lined with ancient books on one wall and with a huge fireplace big enough to roast a hog in. Windows on three sides overlooked the undulating Tuscan landscape, and Justina gave a sigh of pleasure.

'Like it?' asked Dante.

'Who could fail to like it?' She looked at the paintings and the dark furniture, the silken rugs on the cool floor. 'It's the kind of place people dream of visiting.'

He pointed to an open door through which she could see an antique cot on which sat a battered-looking teddy bear.

'Nico's going to go in there. Obviously.' He smiled. 'Would you like to see where we'll be sleeping?'

At first Justina pretended she had misheard him. But her heart started to race as he pushed open an adjoining door, where a large room was dominated by one enormous bed.

'We're sharing a room?' She gave a light laugh. 'Are you serious?'

'Totally serious.' The shrug of his shoulders was unapologetic. 'My mother is making an effort to be mod-

ern, and she has put us in together because she thinks
we're a couple now.'

'And you haven't bothered to enlighten her that we're
not?'

'I haven't told her that we find ourselves here as a
result of a one-night stand, if that's what you mean.'

His assessment was brutal—was that deliberate?—
and it *hurt*. 'How ironic that when we *were* here as a
couple we were at opposite ends of the house,' she observed, swallowing down the sudden lump in her throat.
'Meaning that you had to come creeping into my room
at the dead of night.'

'I don't remember you objecting too much at the
time, *tesoro*. As I recall, the subterfuge rather turned
you on.'

Justina bit back the objection which had sprung to
her lips, because it hadn't been the subterfuge which had
turned her on—it had been *him*. Dante had only used to
look at her and she would be melting with desire. She
met the mockery in his eyes and the sudden flip in her
stomach made her realise that nothing very much had
changed. He could still turn her on with just a look—
and wasn't that *dangerous*, given this new proximity?
On one level she was honest enough to admit to herself
that she was desperate to have sex with him again, but
on another she knew that it would be complete madness.

Nico stirred and she held out her arms for him, relieved to be able to press her burning cheek onto his
downy little head. 'I'd better feed him,' she said.

Dante nodded. He had seen the look of confusion which had clouded her amber eyes and he wondered how hard she was going to fight him. And fight herself. 'Why not go over there?' he said, indicating an old rocking chair which sat in front of one of the windows. 'While I unpack.'

Justina carried Nico over to the window, crooning a little as she did so, before unbuttoning her silk shirt and latching him on to her breast. She'd never sat in a rocking chair before, and the creaking rhythm was oddly soothing. It made her feel timeless—and safe. Dreamily, she stroked the baby's head as he fed, and in the background she could hear the sounds of Dante pulling open drawers and shutting wardrobes.

By the time she was finishing he had returned and was standing watching her. His eyes were as soft and dark as molten jet and suddenly she felt almost shy. But how could she possibly feel *shy* in view of everything that had happened between them?

She tried for flippant instead. 'What do you think you're looking at?'

'At you. You look unbelievable. Like a Madonna. A Madonna in skinny jeans.'

'Will you stop it?' She could feel her cheeks getting hotter by the second. 'I'm busy feeding your son.'

'And you do it so well.'

'It's a biological function, Dante,' she said drily. 'Every woman does it.'

But every woman did *not* do it. Dante knew that. And

once again Justina had surprised him. Hadn't he thought that she would be itching to wean Nico and leave him in the care of a nanny, so that she could concentrate on her songwriting? But she hadn't. She had embraced motherhood with an enthusiasm he could never have envisaged. And wasn't that what made this whole scenario seem almost *miraculous*? Justina sitting in a rocking chair at the D'Arezzo *palazzo*, feeding their baby. She looked light years away from the black-eyed temptress who had once strutted the stage to the appreciative roars of thousands of fans.

He continued to watch as she settled Nico down, but he sensed a certain restraint about her as she moved away from the cot—as if she'd also moved away from her comfort zone. And he didn't want her uptight. He wanted her soft and giving—the way he'd been fantasising about for too long now.

'The bathroom's through there,' he said. 'You might want to go and freshen up.'

Glad to escape from his unsettling scrutiny, Justina went into the bathroom, where she stripped off and stood beneath the warm torrents of water and tried to put Dante out of her mind—easier said than done when desire kept straying into her mind with dark and dangerous thoughts. And she couldn't hide in the shower all day.

She wandered back into the bedroom, clad only in a towel and found Dante standing there, his expression unfathomable as he watched her walk in. She supposed she should say something on the lines of *I didn't know you'd be here*—except that would have been a lie. Where else would he be when they were supposed to be sharing a bedroom?

'Is Nico okay?' she questioned awkwardly.

For a moment he didn't move, and when eventually he nodded Justina could see that his powerful body looked as tense as she felt.

'Fast asleep. Want to see?'

Nodding, she followed him into the adjoining bedroom, where their son lay sleeping in the antique cot, the wood very dark against the pristine whiteness of the bedclothes. For a moment she just stood and watched the steady rise and fall of his little chest, marvelling at the thought of the tiny heart which beat within it and the fact that she and Dante had created this living miracle between them. Out of one reckless act of passion this beautiful little child had been born.

And what of Nico's life? she wondered suddenly. Would he suffer as she had suffered because a man and a woman had come together as she and Dante had done? Not thinking about the consequences of their actions, thinking of nothing but the heat of the moment and the overwhelming lure of desire? Growing up, she had hated her own illegitimacy, and yet now she had bequeathed that same pain to her child.

With a strangled little sound she turned and walked back into the bedroom, scarcely aware that Dante was close behind her. At least not until his hand had reached out to her bare shoulder and was turning her round.

'Justina? What's wrong?'

She shook her head. How could she admit to the great cauldron of insecurity which was bubbling away inside her when all she could think about was the burn of his fingers on her bare flesh?

'*This* is wrong—this whole farce of us coming here with our baby and being put in this room together as if we're all some kind of happy family,' she said desperately, shaking his hand away. '*We're* wrong!'

'No!'

His voice was fierce as he pulled her into his arms, his voice unsteady as he pressed his face close to hers. So close that she could feel the heat of his breath fanning over her skin.

'We have never been wrong. How can it possibly be wrong when it feels like this whenever I touch you?'

'Dante—'

'Kiss me,' he growled. 'And then tell me again that we're wrong. Do that and I'll never lay another finger on you.'

She opened her mouth to say that was cheating. That she didn't want to kiss him. But that would have been a lie. Because hadn't she wanted this all along? Deep down hadn't she been yearning for this—the hard pressure of his kiss and her own urgent response to it? Hungrily, her lips sought his, and he tugged at the towel and let it slither to the floor, so that she was completely naked.

For a moment he pulled away so that he could look at her, sucking in a breath as his gaze burned over her, and she was so lost in the moment and the way he was making her feel that she did nothing. She could feel her nipples springing to life beneath his hungry scrutiny, and the melting desire which was pooling insistently at the fork of her thighs.

'Dante,' she breathed. 'This is…'

'Inevitable,' he bit out, as he began to tug at his belt. 'It's been inevitable for a long time now. Because you are beautiful. The most beautiful woman I have ever seen. And I am aching for you. I am crazy for you, *tesoro.*'

No, *this* was crazy, she thought. Dante was talking with an emotion she hadn't heard in a long time and stripping off his clothes with ruthless efficiency, while she just stood there and watched him! She bit her lip as she saw his erection springing free, and a rush of desire flooded over her as he splayed his hands over her bare hips and pulled her down onto the bed.

'Dante,' she whispered, 'we can't do this.'

'Want to bet?'

'But your family,' she said desperately.

'Dinner isn't for hours.'

'But—'

'No more buts, Justina. Especially when we both

know you don't really mean them. Don't you realise this is siesta time and you're in Italy now?'

His lips were trailing fire as they brushed over her neck and her eyes closed as her head fell back against the pillow. 'Oh,' she said indistinctly.

'I want to kiss every inch of you,' he breathed. 'I want to touch every part of your body. Do you know that?'

Now his finger was stroking its way over her breast, teasing over the aching mound until it alighted with teasing precision on the nipple. 'I… Oh…'

'Your breasts are bigger than they used to be.'

'And do you…do you approve?'

He smiled against her lips. 'Mmm. One hundred percent.'

His finger had moved down over her belly and quickly she sucked it in. 'Dante!'

'Relax. Why are you holding your breath like that?'

'Because my breasts aren't the only things which are bigger. My stomach is *huge*!'

He laid the flat of his hand over the slight cushioning of her flesh. 'Your stomach is perfect. Just as you are perfect.'

'No, I'm not.'

'Will you shut up and come here?'

He bent his head to kiss her and Justina could feel herself almost drowning in the sweetness of that kiss and the things he had just said to her. *He thought she was perfect!* She clung to him as his fingers drifted to her bare knee and then made an almost careless journey up her thigh. He skated teasing little circles there until she was gasping, and then his finger flicked against her sticky heat and she gasped some more. And suddenly his possession became more important than immediate pleasure. She wanted to *feel* him. She wanted him deep inside her again.

'Dante…' she whispered.

'What?' he whispered back.

'Please.'

'Can't wait any longer?'

'N-no.'

'Me neither, *tesoro*. Me neither.'

She held her breath as he moved over her, and the world seemed to stand still as he entered her with one deep and possessive thrust. She felt a great warmth suffuse her, and the breath she'd been holding escaped. She thought she felt him smile against her lips before starting to kiss her again. And Justina let go. Suddenly it was easy to let go. To forget about what had brought them here and concentrate instead on the way he was making her feel.

'Oh,' she breathed again.

Through the dark mists of his own pleasure he managed to get words out. 'Does that hurt?'

'God, no. It feels…incredible.'

'I know it does. For me, too.' He closed his eyes as he lost himself in the rhythm. He'd thought that the sex would be different, and it was—just not in the way he'd imagined. Justina was as tight and delectable as she'd ever been, but it felt... Dante groaned. It felt more than sex had ever felt before. Something which went deeper than physical pleasure. Was that because this body had given birth to his baby—because part of him had grown deep inside her?

He felt her thighs wrap themselves around his back and her fingers digging into his shoulders. He could feel her climax building, and even though he could have come in an instant he held back. He held back even though it nearly killed him—and only when she started to come did he let go and he thought his orgasm was never going to end.

For a while the room was silent, save for the shuddering sounds of air being gulped back into their starved lungs, like two people who had just been saved from drowning. And when their breathing was steady he kissed her for a long time—until the need to yawn became unbearable.

'Charming,' she said, stroking a fingertip over the rasp of growth at his jaw as he opened his eyes and looked at her.

'I do my best,' he murmured.

She could hear the sleepiness in his voice and for a moment Justina lay in the warm circle of his arms and let sensation ripple over her skin. His lips were pressed against her neck, and in that moment she felt utterly protected. She wanted to tell him that nobody else had ever made her feel this way. She wanted to blurt out the secrets she'd held hidden in her heart for so many years.

But Dante had hurt her. He had hurt her badly. Why would she risk that happening all over again? Why jeopardise everything with an emotional outburst when it was far better to play safe? She needed to protect herself against the threat of heartbreak—as much for Nico's sake as for her own. Because a heartbroken mother did not make a good mother. She of all people knew that.

So sleep, she told herself. *Take this opportunity to rest. You're tired, you're a new mother and you've got a family dinner to get through tonight.*

Dante heard the slowing of her breathing as she snuggled against him and he stared down at the ebony hair which spread like treacle over the pillow. He studied the dark curve of her eyelashes and the paper-pale skin against which they brushed. She was pressed so close that he could feel the beating of her heart, and something like certainty crept over him.

He thought about the baby who lay sleeping in the next room. He thought about the harsh and unequivocal words of his lawyer as he acknowledged one fundamental truth. That he wanted this…this family. Just like she'd said, he wanted it all. Nico. Her. All of them together.

And Justina was going to have to start seeing things his way.

CHAPTER NINE

JUSTINA WOKE ALONE from a restless sleep, where images of green mountains were interwoven with the intimate caress of a man's strong body and a silence where there should have been a baby's cry. Startled, she sat bolt upright in bed.

A baby's cry!

Momentarily disorientated, she looked around, trying to get her bearings, blinking back her faint feeling of disbelief. She was in Dante's family villa. More accurately, she was in Dante's bed. She stared down at the empty space beside her. Only he'd gone. Where…?

She jumped out of bed, grabbing at one of the rumpled sheets to wrap it around her naked body before stumbling into the adjoining room to find Nico's cot empty.

A whimper erupted from her throat as she fought to control a rising feeling of panic. Where was her baby? She rushed back into the bedroom and threw on jeans and a sweater, before slipping her feet into a pair of flip-flops as she ran from the room to look for him.

But the *palazzo* was vast, and although she called out Dante and Nico's names in an increasingly concerned voice her calls were met with a resounding silence.

She ran outside, her eyes skating over the horizon, over the distant mountains and the sunlight which was gilding the leaves of the olive trees. Only then did she see him, down among the neat rows of the vines. A tall, dark man pushing a buggy, silhouetted against the classic Tuscan backdrop. Her heart lurched with relief, but she felt the shimmering of something else as she began to run towards them. Something which felt uncomfortably like fear.

'Dante!'

She saw him stop. Saw him lean down as if he was saying something to the inhabitant of the buggy. And then he straightened up and stood, perfectly still, watching her run towards him until she finally reached them, her breath coming in ragged gasps.

'What are you *doing*?' she demanded, her eyes raking over the cot. Her anxiety was only allayed when she saw that Nico was lying there, sleeping peacefully.

Dante heard the breathless accusation in her voice and something inside him hardened. 'What does it look like?' he demanded. 'I brought Nico out for a walk in the fresh air.'

Her fears—which had seemed so real—now began to evaporate. 'I thought…'

'What did you think, Justina?' he questioned acidly. 'That I'd kidnapped our son?'

In the beauty of the Tuscan afternoon her response now seemed faintly ridiculous. 'I woke up alone.'

'I thought you could use the sleep.'

'I've...' She struggled to explain, wanting to wipe that cold, hard look from his face. 'It's all been a bit of an adjustment. Not just coming here, but getting used to having a baby around. This is the first time since he's been born that he hasn't been...' She sucked in a deep breath. 'That he hasn't been there when I've woken.'

Slowly Dante nodded as he acknowledged what lay behind her behaviour, but he also knew that her actions were motivated by something that went much deeper than maternal anxiety. He had never wanted nor asked for the judgement of a woman until now, but for the first time in his life he could see that he needed to give voice to the one question which had remained unspoken.

'Don't you trust me, Justina?' he asked quietly.

Justina looked at him. She knew what she should say. She should tell him that, yes, of course she trusted him—because wouldn't that smooth things over? He would smile, and then they would kiss, and then make a fuss of Nico. And to anyone watching from the house they would look like the perfect family. But this wasn't some sort of play, she reminded herself. This was real life—and being in bed with him this afternoon had made some of her defences come tumbling down. She couldn't keep hiding from the truth simply because it was painful. Dante had asked her an unexpectedly honest question which deserved nothing but an honest answer.

'Actually, no,' she said. 'Not really.'

He stilled, because somehow hadn't he expected—hoped for—a different response? 'So me being there for you during the birth and afterwards counts for nothing?'

Her gaze was steady. 'I didn't realise you were doing it to score Brownie points.'

'I *wasn't*,' he defended, indignation catching in his throat as he looked at her long dark hair which was blowing in the breeze. And suddenly he wanted to make it very clear to her exactly where he stood on the subject of other women. 'Don't you realise that I haven't looked at another woman since I met you again at Roxy's wedding?'

'How would I know that?' she asked quietly. 'I'm not a mind-reader.'

'Let me tell you what it was like when I saw you again after all those years,' he said slowly. 'You blew me away—just like you did before. I couldn't get you out of my mind. I kept telling myself to stay away from you. That we were bad for each other. I knew that. Only the temptation to come and find you was eating away at me.'

She didn't say anything, because his words didn't sound like affection or anything close to it. They sounded like *addiction*. Was Dante addicted to the emotional danger which had always existed between them? Was she?

'And then I discovered you were pregnant,' he said. 'And my desire very quickly became anger. Anger that you didn't bother to tell me. That you were prepared to keep me in the dark about the fact I was going to be a father.'

'Surely you can understand why I did that?'

'Not really, no. Was it power that made you keep it secret?' he questioned. 'Or control?'

Standing silhouetted against the dying apricot light of the Tuscan day, Justina thought that she had never seen him looking more indomitable, and yet his inherent arrogance almost took her breath away.

'I'm amazed you can say all that to me with a straight face,' she said. 'You told me that it was never meant to be anything more than a one-night stand—so why would I foist on you the repercussions of that meeting? You were going to have a baby with a woman you despised. No…please.' She lifted her hand as he opened his mouth to speak. 'Let me finish, because it's important. I thought that a baby would be the last thing you wanted and so I didn't tell you. I can see now that was wrong, but I was trying to be independent.'

'Of course you were.'

She ignored the sardonic note which had hardened his voice. 'I should have given you a choice about how much involvement you wanted instead of assuming that you wanted none.'

'Or was that what *you* wanted, Justina?' His voice

was silky-soft now. 'For me not to have any contact with our child?'

She looked into his eyes. Weren't lies sometimes kinder than the truth? She knew it would be easier all round if she just denied it. Yet she also knew that they had passed the point of twisting the truth in order to spare each other's feelings. 'Of course it's what I wanted,' she said. 'I didn't want you back in my life in any way. You bring with you too many complications, Dante.'

Dante heard the cool determination in her voice and saw the candid gaze from her eyes. Her words hurt far more than he had expected them to, but her honesty was curiously refreshing. It told him exactly where he stood and it told him just what he needed to do. 'I guess that pretty much concludes all we need to say on the subject of paternity,' he said. 'Maybe we should now do something inherently civilised—like going inside to drink some coffee.'

She nodded, shaken by the frankness of the exchange but pleased at the unexpected turnaround which the conversation had taken. 'That sounds exactly what I need.'

As if on cue, Nico began to stir. Justina looked down at him, a fierce love swelling up in her heart as his long lashes fluttered open. 'Hello, you,' she said softly. 'Are you hungry?'

They walked back to the house, where Justina fed and changed Nico, and soon afterwards Dante's mother knocked on the door and asked if she might take the baby to show to the staff.

'And, no, I don't need you to help me!' she said very firmly to her son.

There was a moment of silence once Signora D'Arezzo had gone. The two of them stood listening to the echoing sound of her retreating footsteps, and then Dante turned to Justina and lifted her fingertips to his lips.

'Coffee?' he questioned.

She shivered, all their disharmony dissolved by that first touch. 'If you like.'

'Or bed?'

She told herself that coffee was the safer option—so why was she nodding with that schoolgirl-shy smile and letting him lead her through to the bed, where the sheets were still rumpled from before? She bent to straighten them, but the drift of his fingertips over her bottom halted her.

'Don't,' he said roughly. 'It's a waste of time.'

She turned to face him, and he pushed her down on the bed and began to kiss her.

Some of the tenderness of earlier had gone—had been replaced with an unmistakable urgency. He tugged off her clothes with impatient fingers, and somehow she managed to accomplish the same with his. Their bare bodies met in a warm collision of skin, and Justina felt the instant shock of familiarity and lust. He seemed so powerfully dark and dominant as he moved over her, his carved features rigid with restraint as she touched the hard, silken length of him.

'Don't,' he groaned.

She drifted her fingertips upwards and downwards in a light and teasing motion. 'Sure?'

Eyes glinting, he removed the offending hand, circling it with his fingers and holding it above her head so that she was effectively imprisoned beneath him. He looked so dark and dominant and powerful, she thought. And she was discovering that she liked that. She liked the feeling that this was beyond her control, that she was submitting to Dante's will—because didn't that stop her thinking too deeply about whether or not she should be doing it at all?

Her orgasm came swiftly, and afterwards she drifted in and out of sleep until the clock chimed seven and she forced herself to go and take a shower. The room was very quiet when she returned. Dante was already dressed and fastening a pair of pale gold cufflinks. He glanced up to find her watching him, and he smiled as his gaze took in the white towel which was wrapped around her.

'I'm getting a distinct feeling of *déjà vu*,' he drawled. 'You do realise that you'll have me in a permanent state of arousal if you insist on walking around looking like that?'

She could still feel his heated gaze on her as she went over to the dressing table and sat down. She took a wand of mascara and held it to her eye, but Dante had followed her. He was standing behind her and lifting the dark curtain of damp hair before leaning down to press his lips against the back of her exposed neck.

'You smell delicious.'

'It's only soap.'

'Then it is a very delicious soap.'

She closed her eyes. 'Dante...'

'Mmm?'

'We...we don't have a lot of time before dinner.'

'I know we don't, *tesoro*—but I want you to know that I'm crazy about you. That I want you very much and that we have a lot of making up to do.' His hand splayed over her breast and she opened her eyes to see the erotic image of his dark fingers star-fished over the white towelling reflected back at her in the mirror.

'Just go,' she whispered.

'I'm going—but all through dinner I shall be thinking about how much I am going to enjoy touching you later, just like this.'

She felt a wrench of longing as he moved away, leaving her to apply her make up with fingers which were now trembling and to slip into the new underwear she'd bought. All the time she was aware of him watching her. And somehow he could make her feel more self-conscious than she'd ever been on a stage in front of thousands of people. He made her feel...*exposed*. As if the tough skin she'd formed to protect herself could be stripped away by a single, searing slant of those dark eyes.

Her silk sheath dress was the colour of cappuccino, and she teamed it with a pair of towering nude-coloured shoes. She'd twisted her hair into an elaborate knot, and her only jewellery was a pair of dangling pearl and diamond earrings which sparkled and gleamed against her neck.

'Who bought you those?' he questioned suddenly.

She finished applying lip gloss and turned round as something in the tone of his voice brought a sudden tension into the room. 'Do a woman's jewels always have to be bought for her by somebody else?'

'They usually are when they're as expensive as those ones clearly are.'

There was a pause. 'I bought them myself, if you must know.'

'Of course you did.' He gave a short laugh and his voice took on a hard note, as if he was remembering something. 'The ever-independent Justina Perry.'

'That's me,' she said lightly, but his words hurt—as she suspected they were meant to. Maybe this was a timely reminder that nothing between them had really changed. Before she started allowing herself to believe that it was safe to start loving him again she needed a reality check. Yes, they had the most amazing sex, but underneath he was still the same judgemental man.

'And the jewels which I bought you? What happened to those?'

'I tried to give them back to you.'

'And I told you to keep them. Apart from the ring, of

course—which, as you know, was a family heirloom.'
There was a pause. 'So where are they now?'

Justina wriggled her shoulders uncomfortably. Why couldn't he just let it go? 'I sold them.'

He frowned. 'All of them?'

'There's no need to look at me like that, Dante. I gave the money to charity.'

'I told you to keep them,' he repeated. He remembered a bracelet he'd had specially commissioned—a circlet of yellow diamonds, chosen because they reminded him of her eyes. He remembered the way she had smiled as he'd slipped it onto her wrist, and the dreamy way she'd said that one day their daughter would wear it. So much for her vow that she would treasure it for ever! 'They were bought for you and only you. I don't want some other woman wearing them.'

'Oh, come *on*, Dante.' Should she tell him that the sight of all those baubles had made her heart ache every time she'd looked at them? Jewels which most women would long to own had seemed to represent nothing but failure. They'd reminded her of the man she'd loved and lost—and who could live with that? 'Since when did any woman ever wear stuff given to her by her ex-fiancé?'

The bell rang for dinner, putting an end to their discussion—but Dante found himself remembering one sentence in particular which his lawyer had drummed into him. "Independent women make the worst adversaries in any custody battle, Dante. A needy woman is always much more amenable."

If that was the case then no female on the planet could be more fiercely independent than the one who stood in front of him. 'Come on,' he said abruptly. 'Let's go.'

Justina was aware that his mood was cool as they walked along the stone-flagged corridor, and tentatively she linked her arm through his, wanting him to lose that hard and grim expression. 'So who else will be at dinner?' she questioned softly. 'Apart from your mother.'

'My brother, obviously. You remember Luigi?'

'How could I forget?'

'And my sister has travelled from Rome to be here. My cousins are eager to meet you again, but I felt that it might be a bit much to subject you to mass scrutiny on your first evening. So we'll save that for another day.'

She let go of his arm just before they walked into the main salon, where Dante's brother was throwing a large log onto the fire.

'Hello, Luigi,' Justina said quietly, and he looked up. He was as tall and as powerfully built as his brother, but his skin had the darker glow of someone who spent their life working outside. Dante had told her that Luigi had run the vast estate since the death of their father, and was now one of the world's leading wine experts. She thought that his eyes were cool and watchful as he greeted her.

'Justina,' he said. 'This is an unexpected pleasure.'

She smiled up at him. 'It's good to see you again.'

'Indeed. And I believe I must congratulate you on giving birth to my brother's child?'

'Thank you,' she said, thinking that was a characteristically *possessive* D'Arezzo way of phrasing it.

'Now, what can I get you to drink?'

She was longing for one of the glasses of prosecco which stood on a tray, but she was mindful of the fact that she was breastfeeding—so her nerves would have to remain ruffled. 'Some fizzy water would be perfect.'

At that moment a beautiful girl ran into the room, her arms outstretched in greeting. Giulia D'Arezzo was the only female in the family, and rather more demonstrative than both her brothers, and Justina found herself laughing as she was enveloped in an enthusiastic hug.

'Oh, Jus! I'm so happy to see you again—I can't tell you! I've only just arrived—the traffic from Rome was atrocious. Am I too late to see Nico? Have you put him to bed already?'

'I'm afraid I have—or rather Dante has. Babies of Nico's age seem to spend most of their time sleeping—but we can creep down later and peep at him if you like,' said Justina. 'Giulia, you look wonderful.'

'*Grazie*. And so do you—though your dress is much longer than the ones you used to wear! Why are you blushing when what I say is true? Now, tell me, are you still making sweet music?' Giulia demanded. 'And why did you stop sending me your albums?'

The warmth of Giulia's welcome made Justina relax, as did the flames from the flickering fire. She sipped at her drink, listening to the younger woman's chatter and managing to skirt around the subject of why she'd felt it was best not to let her friendship with Dante's sister continue. Because that would have been impossible, wouldn't it? She'd needed to cut all ties with the D'Arezzo family once he'd called off their engagement.

By the time they sat down to dinner she had begun to feel genuinely hungry—though she was seated next to Luigi, who seemed to have some sort of not-very-hidden agenda going on. He asked her how her songwriting was going, and when she tried to play it down told her that he'd read recently that one of her songs had been at number one in Australia. But he said it as if she'd committed a crime instead of doing something to be proud of.

The pasta course was cleared away and Luigi poured himself a glass of red wine, nodding his head approvingly when she refused the same. 'You are intending to go back to work, I suppose?' he enquired, leaning back in his chair to look at her.

'Well, I need to support myself,' answered Justina equably.

'But surely you have accumulated enough money during your career never to have to work again?'

It was a question she got asked all the time—but people always underestimated how much money you needed to live on for the rest of your life. Justina had seen people lose their fortunes and be left scraping around and had vowed it would never happen to her.

She'd seen for herself what could happen to women who didn't work. She'd seen her own mother clinging to rich men who discarded her when someone younger and prettier came along.

'I have a very strong work ethic,' she said carefully. 'And besides, the work I do is very flexible.'

'I'm sure it is.' Luigi ran a fingertip around the tip of his wine glass. 'But what will happen to Nico while you are occupied with this songwriting of yours? Will you be able to concentrate? Will you hear him above the music if he cries out for his *mamma*?'

'Luigi,' said Dante warningly.

Justina put her glass of water down with a hand which wasn't quite steady. 'Probably not. So I'll just leave him to fend for himself,' she said. 'I can probably arrange the baby equivalent of a cat-flap. You know—a saucer of milk, maybe a rusk or two. He can just crawl in and out and help himself.'

Luigi pushed his glass away and said something to his brother in a low stream of Italian—a statement clearly designed to exclude her. But Justina was listening carefully enough to register some of the words. She saw the look which hardened Dante's face before he made a furious response which was too rapid for her to understand.

Forcing herself to pick at food she didn't want, she was glad when the meal ended and she could fulfil her promise to Giulia by taking her to see the baby. But her

heart was aching as they walked into Nico's bedroom
to where he lay sleeping.

He was swaddled inside the cot and Giulia stared
down at him for a long moment. Her voice was a breathless whisper when eventually she spoke. 'Oh, but he is
beautiful, Justina. Absolutely beautiful.'

'I know he is.' Justina felt the stupid lump which rose
in her throat as they stood there, and her fierce sense
of maternal pride was blotted out by the terrible sense
that nothing was really as it should be. That everything
was so damned *complicated*.

But she managed a smile as she and Giulia moved
away. 'Tomorrow you shall hold him as much as you
like. I might even let you change his nappy if you behave yourself!'

Giulia was still laughing when they returned to the
dining room, where coffee was being served, and Justina took the opportunity to excuse herself before slipping back to their suite.

She fed and changed Nico and put him back in his
cot, and was standing in her silk robe, staring out at
the starry night sky, when she heard Dante enter the
room behind her.

She didn't turn round immediately. Just said in a
flat and emotionless voice, 'What was Luigi saying to
you over dinner?'

There was a pause. 'We spoke of many things, Justina. You were there, remember?'

At this, she turned round—her body automatically

responding to the way he was removing his tie and unbuttoning his silk shirt to reveal a triangle of dark, honed chest beneath. *Keep it real,* she reminded herself. *Don't let yourself be swayed by how much you want him.*

'I listened to him insulting me by implying that I was a neglectful mother. I know that.'

'And I put him right. I told him that you are a brilliant mother.'

'Did you?'

'Certainly I did. I said that no mother could be more devoted nor more loving than you are.'

That took the wind right out of her sails. She didn't want Dante praising her because that was distracting. She wanted to get to the bottom of what Luigi had been saying. 'I'm thinking more specifically about when he spoke to you in Italian.'

'I don't remember.'

'You don't? That's quite unusual for a man with your sharp sense of recall, Dante. Perhaps I'd better jog your memory for you. He said *matrimonio*—which means marriage, and which I imagine is understandable in most languages. But he also said *avoccato.*' She frowned. 'Which means lawyer, if my memory of my Italian classes serves me well.'

There was a moment of silence before Dante spoke. '*Brava, tesoro,*' he said softly. 'I had no idea you were so advanced in my language.'

'Please don't patronise me, Dante. Just tell me what you were talking about.'

For a moment he didn't answer, and there was no sound other than the faint clatter of metal on wood as he put his cufflinks down on the dresser. He had intended to say this to her, yes—but not in this way. Not as something produced as a defence against a heated accusation made at the end of a long day. He had planned to wait until she had softened. Until he had made love to her and she was lying in his arms in one of those rare moments when he sensed she might be close to letting her carefully built defences fall away.

He met the amber fire in her eyes. 'I had planned to ask you to marry me.'

CHAPTER TEN

JUSTINA FLINCHED, THINKING how *wrong* Dante's words sounded. It was the coldest marriage proposal she could have imagined—and how it mocked her. The first time he'd asked her to be his wife he had been brimming over with love—but now his voice was completely different. It was like playing a familiar piece of music and discovering that the disc was covered with dust, so that the sound came out all distorted.

'Right,' she said, somehow managing to keep her voice steady. 'That's why your brother mentioned matrimony. But that wasn't all you were talking about, was it? I'm interested to know why you mentioned lawyers. It's not usually a top topic for dinner conversation—particularly as you both switched to speaking in Italian.'

Dante's eyes narrowed, because surely she knew him well enough to realise that he would have covered this particular base. And if she was missing the point then wasn't it time he enlightened her?

'I've spoken to my lawyer,' he said. 'Obviously.'

'Oh, *obviously*,' she echoed sardonically. 'And what did your lawyer say?'

'She advised me that in our particular situation marriage would be the best solution.'

She? Justina nodded. Of course Dante would have a female lawyer—*of course he would!* 'But a solution implies some sort of problem.'

'*Si!*' he agreed hotly. 'There *is* a problem! A big problem. Surely you can see that for yourself? We have different lives but a shared child. And for as long as we remain unmarried I have no legal say in what happens to that child.'

He felt his lips harden with determination. What had his lawyer said? *"Marriage just makes things easier, Dante—because even if the marriage doesn't endure the law is on your side. Without it you must rely on the woman's benevolence in order to see your child—and this woman might not be feeling particularly benevolent towards you."*

He looked at Justina now, her black hair silvered by the moonlight which streamed in through the unshuttered windows. He thought how majestic she looked, with the flow of her satin robe clinging like oil to the soft curves of her body. He thought of her talent and the loving way she was with his son.

'Marry me, Justina,' he said.

There was a long silence as Justina looked into his eyes and tried to steel herself against their dark beauty. She told herself that this was not the time to listen to her heart—that the soft dip in his voice was simply Dante at his most charmingly manipulative. For her son's sake she had to be governed by reason and nothing else.

'And if I do. What's in it for me?' she questioned.

'Security, of course.' He smiled. 'And family.'

Justina smiled back, because he was clever. Oh, he was *very* clever. He had picked on the two things which had always eluded her. The two things she'd always yearned for. A sense of home and being rooted and a sense of being safe. But how could she be safe when what they had was only the mirage of a family… And once that mirage had disappeared, what would be left behind? A man who didn't love and a woman who did.

She shook her head, fighting against the temptation to leap at it, telling herself that she had too much to lose by buying into a dream. 'It isn't enough.'

'Why not?'

'Because…' And then the words came tumbling out. Words she'd buried in some deep place inside herself now spooled out in a dark stream. 'Because I can't be married to a man I don't trust. A man who can just walk away from a woman he was supposed to marry and a few short days later take somebody else to his bed!'

He winced. 'What's the point of bringing that up again?' he questioned wearily. 'I thought we'd done all this. It's in the past, Justina. It's done.'

'But the legacy of that day continues, Dante. It threatens any future we might have—can't you see that?'

'No, I damned well can't. Our relationship was *over*,'

he bit out. 'You know that. I wasn't expecting you to walk in on me. That was the last thing in the world I wanted.'

'But that's not the point, is it? The point is that you were....you were with *her*.' Briefly she covered her mouth, as if she was afraid she might be sick, before letting her fingers slide down to rest against her neck. 'I thought what we had was so special—but how could it have been? How the hell could you replace me so quickly?'

'She was not *replacing* you! She could never have replaced you. Nobody could. I know it was wrong. God help me, I know that now. But I was hurting. And I missed you,' he said simply. 'I missed you so much.'

'You had a funny way of showing it.'

'And I was angry,' he admitted. 'More angry than I'd ever been. That played its part—of course it did. I was angry that you kept going away on tour—that you were prepared to put your career before our relationship. I guess I blamed you for the split, and I did what countless other men have done in the same situation. I went to a bar and drank a little too much, and she—'

'*I don't want to hear this!*'

'Well, maybe you should!' His black eyes burned into her. 'Maybe it should all come out so that we can be rid of it once and for all. She came on to me like women are always coming on to me—only I'd never looked at another woman from the moment I'd met you. It was never even a consideration. Only this time it was different. We were over. Finished. This time I wanted...comfort.'

'Stop it!' she hissed. 'You wanted sex and you damned well got it! You were just unlucky that I came in and caught you.'

'I was *wrong*,' he repeated harshly. 'I just grabbed at the first thing which came along and it was too soon—much too soon. And if its purpose was to try to forget you, then I can assure you that it didn't work.'

'It's easy to say that now.'

'*Easy*? You think this is easy?' he demanded, his face so tense that it looked as if it might shatter at any moment. 'If I could go back in time I would. If I could change it then I would. But I can't. Nobody can do that.' His eyes were the colour of molten jet as he held both hands up in a gesture of appeal. 'I'm asking you to forgive me, Jus. I'm asking you to take me back and to marry me—to let me spend the rest of my life making you happy.'

Justina's heart contracted with a pain which was complicated by a temptation so strong that she didn't know if she'd be able to resist it. Because she *wanted* to reach out and tell him that, yes, she would take him back. She *wanted* to have him hold her and kiss her and keep her close. She *wanted* to buy in to the dream that they could be the perfect couple and the perfect family. But it *was* just a dream—how could it be anything other than that when the trust between them had been severed?

He said that he wanted only her—but he'd said that once before, hadn't he? Who was to say that Dante wouldn't stray next time they ran into some kind of difficulty, as inevitably they would? There were a million women out there, just waiting to "come on" to him. She knew that. There was always a woman waiting in the wings for a married man to have a weak enough moment to stray. Hadn't her own mother proved that, time and time again?

And through all his extraordinary declaration—through all his heartfelt words—there remained one startling omission. He hadn't even mentioned the word *love*. Maybe she should be grateful that he wasn't coating his proposal with sweet declarations which meant nothing, but what hope would a marriage have *without* love? Even if she was honest enough to admit to herself that she was falling in love with him all over again that wouldn't be enough to go round, would it? Not nearly enough to protect her from the influence of gorgeous blondes with hunger in their eyes.

She forced herself to say it, even though her heart was sending out a silent scream of protest.

'I can't do it,' she said. 'I just...*can't*. I saw it and I felt so utterly *betrayed*—and I don't think I can get past that. Trust is almost impossible to repair once it's been broken.'

'Justina—'

'No. Please, Dante. I promise I will give you reasonable access to your son, but no more than that. I won't marry you—but that doesn't mean we can't be good parents.' At this she stopped and drew in a deep breath which seemed to scorch her lungs, before managing a smile. 'And I don't see any reason why we can't continue to have a perfectly amicable relationship.'

There was a long pause—so long that for a moment she wondered if he'd heard her. But one look at the expression on his face told her that he had. His features seemed to have been carved from stone; they were hard and unmoving. The silence in the room was tense as Justina waited to see how he would respond—and she was surprised when he walked over to her and caught hold of her, pulling her into his body in a single fluid movement. Through her silk robe she could feel the jut of her breasts pushing against his chest, and instantly she felt an inevitable rush of desire which was quickly followed by a hot wave of relief. He didn't mind! He understood her reservations!

For a moment he stared down at her, and his hand moved down over the fall of her hair before coming to alight on one silk-covered breast. She sucked in a breath of anticipation.

'And this "amicable" relationship of which you speak,' he murmured. 'You don't think that's going to be problematic?'

She spoke with more conviction than she felt. 'It doesn't have to be.'

'Do you have any ideas about how we're going to go about it?'

'We could…we could make it up as we go along.'

'Could we?' His smile was cold. 'So how about we start with something like this?'

He slipped his hand inside her robe to cover the breast which had been straining for his touch. She felt his thumb flick over the nipple and she swallowed.

'Yes,' she breathed, scarcely able to get the word out. *'Yes.'*

'So while we are being good parents, and being *reasonable* about access, we will continue to enjoy sex—is that what you are suggesting?'

His tone was a honeyed murmur, even if his words sounded a little on the bald side. 'Yes,' she repeated. 'Definitely.'

His thumb caressed one straining bud. 'You want to do it now, I think?'

Justina swayed. 'You know I do,' she moaned.

The hand was removed with almost clinical efficiency, and Justina didn't even realise that she'd had her eyes closed until she fluttered them open to see the look of naked fury on his face.

'You really think that I would tolerate an arrangement like that? To be treated like some common *stud*? In your dreams, Justina,' he said savagely, and walked out of their bedroom with a soft slamming of the door.

For a moment she stood staring blankly after him, until she realised she was shivering, so she climbed into bed and waited for him to return. It took several sleepless hours before it dawned on her that that he wasn't planning on returning. At least not until after a pale dawn had streaked the Tuscan sky and she'd finished tending to Nico.

Dante walked into the room wearing the same formal trousers he'd had on at dinner, and he had clearly just pulled his dress shirt on over his bare chest, though he hadn't bothered to do it up. His feet were bare, too—and his dark hair was ruffled and untidy.

'Where have you been?' she questioned tiredly.

He gave her a look composed in equal measures of ice and fury. 'Where do you think? We're in the middle of the Tuscan countryside—there aren't really a lot of options open! I slept somewhere else, Justina—there are plenty of available rooms.'

She swallowed, telling herself to stay calm. That nothing could be gained from another angry exchange. 'Why did you storm out like that?'

'*Why?*' he repeated, a look of incredulity darkening his face. 'You really need to ask me that? I asked you to marry me and you said no—but your refusal came with an interesting suggestion.' He gave a bitter laugh before he shot the words out as if he was firing them from a pistol. 'Don't you think it insults me that I'm good enough to *service* you any time you want, good enough to be your stud, just not good enough to be your husband?'

For a moment Justina's resolve wavered. She wanted to blurt out the truth. To tell him that marriage without love wasn't enough, and she was terrified her heart would get broken all over again. But that might sound like a clumsy attempt at emotional bargaining. He might feel cornered into telling her he loved her in order to appease her—and then what? Wouldn't something like that backfire on them in the end?

She pushed her hair behind her ears and surveyed him, her calm expression belying the painful thunder of her heart. 'So what are we going to do?'

'Do?' He pulled off his shirt and hung it over the back of the chair. 'We're going to do exactly what we came here to do. We are going to introduce Nico to the rest of his D'Arezzo family and show him a little Tuscan hospitality and then we will return to England.'

And that, it seemed, was that. End of subject.

Justina was forced to watch as Dante took off his trousers and his underpants. She wanted to avert her eyes as more and more honed olive flesh was revealed, but pride wouldn't let her. Only when he was completely and magnificently naked did he glance up and meet her gaze, his dark eyes mocking her.

'Frustrating, isn't it, *tesoro*? You can look, but you can't touch.'

'I don't want to touch you.'

'*Liar.*'

The soft word sliced through her.

'But let me tell you this, so that there can be absolutely no misunderstanding. That there will be no more *performing* for your pleasure. You don't want me as a husband then you don't get me at all. None of me.'

It was a depressing way to begin the day, but Justina did her best not to let it show because she knew that streams of D'Arezzo cousins were coming over later. And she wanted to salvage something from this trip. Her relationship with Dante might have taken a nose-dive, but she wanted his family to approve of her as a mother, even if it was too much to hope for that they might actually *like* her.

She was aware that some of the cousins were a little wary around her when they arrived just before lunch-time—but she was also aware they'd been at an impressionable age the last time she'd visited. She'd probably seemed distant to them and, if she was being truthful, she had *felt* a little distant. She remembered that while she'd been here her management had rung almost non-stop and it had driven Dante to despair. A photographer had even managed to penetrate the grounds of the family estate and a furious Luigi had threatened to punch him, before sending him on his way.

She didn't miss that side of fame one bit, she realised. The irony was that in many ways she felt much more grounded—and Nico was partly responsible for that. She knew that she would make a better wife now than she would have done at the height of her fame. But she also knew that she couldn't opt for an empty marriage.

Instead, she did her best to fit in with the family—and to her surprise it proved easier than she had anticipated. But then, it was easy to join in with the general clucking over Nico and agree with the sentiment that he was the most beautiful baby in the world! Quickly she realised the significance of this lusty little boy—the first of a new generation of D'Arezzos.

She'd made the biggest effort of all with Beatrix D'Arezzo—wanting her to know that she would do everything and anything for her beloved grandson. So when it came to leaving Dante's mother hugged her tightly, with an affection which did not seem feigned and Justina felt unexpectedly choked, having to swallow down an unexpected lump in her throat as their car arrived to take them to the airport.

She felt deflated on the flight back to England, and not just because the D'Arezzo family's warmth contrasted so bitterly with Dante's new coolness towards her. Now that nobody else was around he seemed to have dropped his politely solicitous attitude towards her. And that didn't bode very well for the future, did it? They were both going to have to override their feelings and think of Nico's welfare.

She stared at him. The plane was lavishly equipped, and he was opposite her, working on a large pile of papers. A lock of black hair had fallen onto his forehead and her fingers itched to brush it away.

'I think the visit went well,' she ventured.

He looked up, his eyes focussing on her almost as if he'd forgotten she was there, and Justina found herself reflecting that a look like that could be more hurtful than all the rage in the world.

'On many levels, yes. I think so, too,' he agreed.

'You'll…you'll be going back to New York, I suppose?'

At this he pushed away the smooth tablet of his computer and studied her with an odd kind of smile. 'That's what you'd like, is it, Justina?'

Justina shrugged. What she'd *like* would be for him to stop sulking. She wanted things to go back to the way they'd been before he'd spoilt it all by asking her to marry him.

'I don't think what I'd like is really relevant,' she said. 'I just assumed you'd be going home.'

'Haven't you learned by now that it's never wise to make assumptions when you're dealing with a D'Arezzo man?' His voice had deepened to a note of dark silk. 'As it happens, I won't be going to New York—no.'

'You won't?' she questioned lightly. 'Why not?'

'Because I'm moving to London.'

She blinked. 'But you work in New York!'

'These days I can work anywhere. That's the beauty of modern communication.'

'But you don't have anywhere to live! Unless you're planning on staying at the Vinoly long-term?'

'A hotel suite is not ideal for a young baby,' he said. 'Which is why I intend on buying a house.'

'You're *what*?'

'With a garden,' he continued. 'Somewhere Nico can sit outside in the fresh air during his access visits.'

'Access visits?' she whispered.

'Of course. Or did you think that they were going to

be on your territory and on your terms? Oh, you *did*?' He gave a disdainful smile as he unclipped his seat belt and stretched out his long legs. 'You know, for someone who has always accused *me* of being the ultimate control freak, you're doing a pretty good impersonation of one yourself, Justina.'

Justina felt spooked. When she'd spoken of access visits back in Tuscany they had been hypothetical. They'd sounded as unthreatening as a dentist's appointment when you knew it was a whole year away. But this...

Dante was moving to London and he was getting a house!

The child in her wanted to scream. She wanted to tell him that she was scared. Scared he would create a *proper* home simply because he knew how to and she didn't. That Nico would grow up preferring to go round to Papa's, while she...

'Miss Perry?'

She'd been so lost in her thoughts that Justina hadn't realised Dante was no longer there. One of the glamorous D'Arezzo stewardesses was standing over her, her perfectly plucked eyebrows raised in question and Justina turned her head just in time to see Dante disappearing into the cockpit. 'Yes?'

'Signor D'Arezzo has decided to land the plane himself, so he's gone in to join the pilot. Would you care to fasten your seat belt?'

Justina felt even more wrong-footed as the stewardess checked that Nico was properly clipped in. What the hell was Dante doing, landing the damned plane? She hadn't even known he could fly!

She glared as he exited the cockpit after a butter-smooth landing. 'I suppose you've learned to walk on water, too?' she questioned acidly.

'Now, now, Justina,' he chided. 'Shouldn't your role be to congratulate me and to tell Nico what a talented daddy he has?'

She didn't trust herself to answer—just felt an increasing swirl of frustration as they prepared to leave the plane. This wasn't how it was supposed to be—although when she stopped to think about it what had she imagined would happen? That Dante would just disappear into the ether, only appearing at Christmas and birthdays, with a smile on his face and a gift in his hand?

Even so, they were halfway back to London before she had plucked up enough courage to ask, 'When do you anticipate moving to London?'

'Straight away,' he replied, shrugging his shoulders with the lazy gesture of someone who could afford to do exactly what he wanted. 'Why wait? I've had my people look into availability, and I'm taking a house in Spitalfields which isn't too far from you. A rather beautiful Georgian house in a glorious green square, as it happens.' He tapped his finger on his laptop. 'Would you like to see some photos?'

Justina felt queasy. 'I'll pass, thank you.'

Her apartment felt soulless and bare after the faded splendour of the Tuscan *palazzo*. She stood in the centre of the oatmeal sitting room while Dante put down her suitcase and thought how *gorgeous* he looked in his dark suit. And about as accessible as a remote and icy mountain peak.

She fiddled with the button of her jacket. 'Dante?'

He bent to drop one final kiss on top of his sleeping son's head, unprepared for the savage twist of pain he felt at the thought of having to say goodbye. Straightening up, he looked into her wide amber eyes and felt the twist of something else, too. Did she know how far she had pushed him and how close he was to snapping?

'Justina?' he said, striving for a neutrality which was only hanging by a thin thread.

'Can't we…?' *Say it,* she urged herself. *Just say it.* 'Can't we still be friends, at least?'

At that moment he could have gone over there and shaken her. Why was she so damned stubborn? Why couldn't she see what was staring her in the face?

With an effort he fought against the slow burn of rage. 'I'm not sure whether we can ever be *friends,*' he said. 'Not in the circumstances. But I'm hopeful that we can achieve the amicable relationship you said you wanted.'

Justina only just managed not to wince. Had she really been stupid enough to demand something like that?

Because why on earth would she want something which now filled her with such dark foreboding?

CHAPTER ELEVEN

THINGS BEGAN TO go wrong the moment Justina got back to England. It started when the lift in her apartment block broke down and for the next two days, until it was mended, she had to lug everything up and down seven flights of stairs. It might have been simpler if she'd swallowed her pride and asked Dante for help, but she was so determined not to rely on him in any way that she said nothing—just kept reflecting on the fact that he had been right all along and this apartment really was no place to bring up a baby.

It got worse when her breast milk dried up—and she was eaten up with guilt as a result. The midwife told her it sometimes happened as a result of stress, and that she wasn't to beat herself up about it, but that was easier said than done. Justina's emotions seemed to be veering all over the place. She felt a failure as a woman and now a failure as a mother.

And wasn't she missing Dante like crazy? Didn't the memory of his closeness taunt her to the point of pain when she lay in bed at night, wondering why she felt so empty inside? Hadn't she been left thinking that the "right" decision now seemed all wrong?

She had only managed not to cry during a midwife's visit by the simple expedient of rubbing her balled fists against her eyes, and it wasn't until Dante arrived soon after and started frowning at her face that Justina glanced in the mirror and saw that her mascara-smudged eyes had left her looking like a panda.

'What's happened?' he demanded. 'Is it Nico?'

'No. Yes. Well, in…in a way.' She swallowed. 'I'm not…I'm not producing any breast milk, and the midwife says that I'm to give him a bottle from now on.'

For a moment his eyes softened, and so did his voice. 'That's a real pity, Justina.'

'Yes.' She nodded. For a moment she thought that he was going to reach out and pull her into his arms, and how she wished he would. All she wanted was to lay her head on his shoulder and howl her heart out so that some of this horrible emptiness might go away. She wanted to lose herself in his powerful embrace and have him tell her that everything was going to be all right, and this time around she might be prepared to believe him.

But he did nothing like that. He just gave her arm the kind of gentle pat he might have administered to an aging family pet. 'Babies survive brilliantly on formula milk,' he reassured her.

Hopefully, she looked at him. She'd forgotten that he'd read just about every book which had ever been written on the subject. 'Do they?'

'Of course they do. And in a way this might make things easier.'

'Easier?' Justina blinked at him. 'How's that?'

'Well, up until now the fact that Nico relies solely on you has governed our timetable, hasn't it? But now he'll be able to come over and spend the night with me. It'll free you up to do some work. Especially now that my new house is looking so good.' He smiled. 'I've had a nursery installed.'

It was appalling that in the middle of such disruption and change and worry about her baby Justina should feel completely redundant and *jealous*. But she did. 'You're sure you don't want any input from me?' she questioned. 'About the nursery, I mean?'

'No, thanks,' he answered coolly. 'I have plenty of ideas of my own.'

She forced a stoic smile. 'Right.'

It got worse.

The first time Nico was due to spend the night with Dante, Justina got him ready with everything he needed for his first overnight trip away. She was trying to push off the heavy blanket of sadness which had fallen over her and to quell her own rising sense of nervousness— not least because they'd arranged she should take him over there herself. She had planned to dress up for her first visit to Dante's new home. Maybe wear that cashmere dress he'd never seen, with her hair hanging loose and a pair of decent shoes. She was going to make sure that she looked *amazing*. She hadn't dared ask herself why such action seemed important, because she was afraid of setting herself up for something which might ultimately fail.

But now the doorbell was ringing, and instead of a cashmere dress and sexy shoes she was wearing jeans and a T-shirt liberally smeared with mashed banana. She opened the door to see Dante standing there, his dark hair windswept and his tie loosened a little at the neck. He looked formal, yet rumpled, and quite ridiculously sexy, and she had never felt more unattractive in her life.

'I'm supposed to be dropping him round to *you*,' she protested, wiping away the little beads of sweat which were inconveniently forming at her forehead.

'I know that—but I had a meeting nearby and so I thought I'd save you the journey.'

'But…but I wanted to see the new nursery.'

There was a pause. 'You can see it another time.'

She recognised the blocking tactic and her smile froze. *He didn't want her there.* Had her refusal to marry him backfired in the most spectacular way possible? Had she pushed him so far away that there was to be no coming back?

She thought she saw him glance at his watch. 'You seem in a hurry to get away!' she said brightly. 'Can't I persuade you to stay and have a coffee before you go?'

Levelly, he met her gaze. 'I don't think that's such a good idea, do you?'

She looked into the flat expression in his eyes and flinched. 'No,' she said hollowly. 'I suppose it isn't.'

'So why don't I just take Nico and leave you to have a well-earned rest?' He lifted his eyebrows. 'Planning on doing something special on your first night of freedom, are you?'

From some dark and lonely place deep inside her she produced a grimace of a smile. 'I haven't decided,' she lied, as if she had a million different options open to her.

'Well, have a good one, whatever it is. And I'll see you tomorrow.'

The apartment felt so quiet after they'd gone, and so *empty.* She prowled around the big modern rooms as if she was looking for something—she just wasn't sure what that something was. The giant mirror in the bedroom gave her a glimpse of her hair, which was sticking to her clammy brow, and she thought it was no wonder that Dante hadn't been able to wait to get away. But she knew that it was about much more than her looking as if she'd been dragged through a hedge twice over. She had thrown his offer of marriage back in his face and in doing that had wounded his pride—perhaps for ever.

She showered and put on a robe, but still she couldn't settle to anything. She supposed she should eat something, but there was very little in the fridge apart from two fat-free yogurts and half a bar of chocolate. She hadn't been eating sensibly and she was going to have to start.

This is what it's going to be like from now on, she

told herself grimly. *This is your future and it's only going to get worse.* She had let fear stop her from taking what she really wanted. Too scared to embrace the start of a brand-new life, she was going to have to sit back and watch while Dante forged a future with someone else. Because sooner or later he would meet a woman. Someone who would love him as a man like him would always be loved. Who would learn to love Nico, too. Why, her beloved son might one day call another woman Mamma.

'No!' Justina shouted forcefully, as if there was someone else in the room to hear her. And then, because it felt so liberating, she shouted it again. *'No!'*

Her hands were trembling as she ran into her bedroom and pulled on some clothes. Then she dashed outside to find a cab, giving Dante's address in Spitalfields in a voice which was shaking.

The air was unseasonably warm and the rush-hour traffic had died away. She stared out of the cab window as they grew closer to his home. Much of the area had been rejuvenated, and everything seemed to be bursting with life. She could see mothers with buggies and the colourful sign for a local nursery school, festooned with bumble-bees and butterflies. Despite its inner-city location it seemed a homely area, and much more suitable for a baby than her sleek apartment block, where she didn't even know a single neighbour.

Nerves threatened to assail her as the cab drew up outside an imposing black front door. She could see lights blazing from a first-floor room. She could hear birds singing in the nearby garden square as she paid her fare, and her thumb was trembling as she jammed it onto the doorbell.

The sound of footsteps warned her that Dante was about to open the door, and when he did she saw a fleeting look of surprise on his face and—yes—annoyance, too. And something else—some dark emotion underpinning all that unwelcoming sternness. Suddenly she wondered what she was doing here—and whether she should chase after that cab and get back inside.

'What is it?' he demanded.

'Am I...' she forced herself to say it '...disturbing you?'

He wanted to say yes, that she had been disturbing him from the first moment he'd met her, when she'd turned those incredible amber eyes on him and he had been lost. But he was through with chasing after Justina and rainbows which didn't exist.

Instead, he fixed her with a questioning look. 'What do you want?'

She sucked in a deep breath. 'Can I come in?'

Wordlessly, he held open the door. She walked past him, and although he was close enough for her to reach out and touch, his body language was so forbidding that he might as well have been on a different planet.

'I'm upstairs,' he said.

For a moment she thought he meant that he was in bed, but as she followed him upstairs she realised it was one of those tall town houses where the sitting room was situated on the first floor.

The scene which greeted her was curiously cosy. A half-drunk glass of red wine stood next to an open newspaper and the sound of Puccini was filling the room. He had hung several huge oil-paintings on the walls and bought furniture so stylish that it must be Italian. It looked like *home*, she thought wistfully. The kind of home she'd always known he would be able to create.

She wanted to go and sink into that squashy-looking sofa and have Dante join her there, pour her some wine—but the dark expression on his face told her that wasn't going to happen.

'What are you doing here?' he questioned.

She could have blurted out a hundred conventional responses to that bald query. She could have told him she wanted to check that Nico was okay. That she wanted to see his house and the way he lived. All of those things were true, but none of them was the real reason why she was here, and somehow she knew she had to find the courage to tell him what that was.

'I'm here because I miss you.'

'You mean you miss the sex,' he said cruelly.

'No. I miss you. *You*.'

'I find that very difficult to believe.'

'But it's *true*! It's true, Dante,' she finished quietly.

'I'm sorry.' He shook his head. 'Flattering as it is that you should feel that way, I'm afraid that I can't do the kind of relationship you want, Justina. I told you that. I'm not interested in being your "friend with benefits". I asked you to marry me and you threw it back in my face.'

'Because I was being naïve—I was wishing for the stars!' she burst out. 'You never told me that you loved me, and I thought that marriage without love wouldn't stand a chance.' She drew in a deep breath. 'But I'm prepared to concede that I was wrong. Because we're doing this for Nico. I realise that. And if it boils down to marrying you or losing you then I'll marry you tomorrow.'

There was a long pause while his eyes captured hers, as if they were searching for a fundamental truth, and suddenly he knew that there was no turning back. No playing safe or covering his back any more. If he wanted her—*really* wanted her—then he had to have the courage to tell her what he hadn't dared admit until now. Not even to himself. That some things never changed and the most important things never should.

'Not just for Nico,' he said slowly. 'I thought it was, but it's not. My lawyer told me that marriage was the only thing to guarantee my role in his life. But when I stopped to think about it afterwards, I knew there was no way that I would tie my destiny to a woman if I didn't love her. No way I could tolerate a whole lifetime with a woman I didn't care about. I have only ever loved one woman, Justina—and that woman is you. I thought that love had died, but it hadn't. It came springing back to life when you had my baby.'

She realised that the music had stopped and that her

rapid breathing was the only sound she could hear. She stared at him, wanting desperately to believe him but still not quite daring to. 'Then why…why didn't you tell me that when you asked me to marry you?'

'Would you have believed me?' His eyes narrowed. 'Didn't you believe we'd spoken of love so often in the past that we had devalued the words by our actions? I wanted the chance to show you that I loved you rather than tell you. But even that won't work if you aren't prepared to forgive me. And I'm not sure you can.'

She felt the ice-cold clench of fear as she heard an awful finality creep into his voice. 'Please don't say any more.'

'I'm going to say it, because you need to hear it.'

'Dante—'

'I know your mother made bad choices. I know you grew up believing that men could never be relied on. And I know I made a mistake—a big mistake.' He lifted his shoulders. 'But if you can't learn to forgive—not just me, but your mother—then the rest of your life is going to be shadowed by the past. Can't you see that? Can't you just let it all go, Jus, and allow yourself to be free?'

And that was when the tears started. Tears she seemed to have been keeping at bay for most of her life. Tears she'd never been allowed to cry as a little girl in case Mummy's boyfriends would think she was troublesome. She'd learnt early that she needed to be strong. To present a cool façade to the outside world and make like she didn't care. She remembered that long night in a hotel suite when she'd been eight—the first time her mother hadn't returned home. She'd lain trembling with terror in bed. And by the morning something had changed. She had survived—she *could* survive— and she could do it on her own. What other choice had there been but to take that forward into her adult life? To forge the independence which had been her one and only anchor and to cling to it?

'I'm sorry,' she sobbed. 'But I was scared, Dante. So scared. And it was a long time since I'd felt that way. My career was the only solid thing I'd ever had and I was afraid that if I let it go—if I learnt to lean on you and rely on you—it would make me vulnerable. That it would all come crashing down around me.' She shuddered in a breath and wiped her wet cheek with her fist. 'The stupid thing was that it all came crashing down in any case.'

'I should never have tried to hold you back,' he said slowly. 'I see that now. I should have realised that your talent and your career were all part of the woman I loved, and that trying to stop you from exploring your potential was like putting a bird into a cage. I should have realised you needed to spread your wings.'

'I have done,' she said huskily. 'I went on the flight of my life. Only now I'm tired of flying and I've discovered that I need somewhere to come home, to roost.'

He stared at her for a minute which seemed like an hour before letting go of a sigh which seemed to come from deep, dark place inside him. Then he opened his arms.

'You've found it,' he said simply. 'I'm right here.'

Her heart missed a beat as she stared at him, knowing that this was crunch time. That if she took those few small steps then she really would have to leave the past behind for ever. 'Dante...' she whispered.

'There is just one more thing, and it's probably the most important thing of all.' His lips softened as every fibre in his being ached to touch her. But he knew that she had to come to him. He could not take from her what she needed to give to him freely. 'I love you. You do realise that?'

She read the truth in the molten depths of his black eyes and her heart turned over with longing. 'Oh, Dante,' she whispered back. 'Darling, darling Dante. I love *you*. I tried so hard not to—but I couldn't seem to stop myself.'

He started laughing. 'Then what the hell are you doing over there?'

She moved almost without realising it, until he was holding her, and she was kissing his lips and his nose and his eyelids, and tears were welling up in her eyes and dripping down her cheeks.

'I'm safe now,' she whispered.

He closed his eyes against her silken hair and let her cry as he knew she needed to. He let her cry until there were no tears left, and then he gently pushed her in the direction of the bathroom and told her to go and wash her face. When she returned, she found him on the sofa, with two glasses of red wine on the table before him, and it was as if he'd read her mind—for wasn't this scene what she'd longed for when she'd first walked in?

She walked over and sat on his lap, facing him, before lowering her head to kiss him. She kissed him tenderly. Deeply and slowly. She kissed him with all the love she'd been holding back until she felt him smile against her lips, and when she pulled away he gave a mock-groan.

'Just one more thing,' she said.

'Hurry up,' he grumbled. 'I want you in my bed within the next ten minutes.'

'It's about all those men I told you I slept with.'

His face darkened. 'I am doing my best to be a tolerant and modern man,' he warned. 'But there is a limit, *tesoro.*'

Ignoring his scowl, Justina wriggled her shoulders. 'Well, they don't exist. I made them up.'

'What do you mean, you made them up?'

'Just that.' She shrugged as she met the dawning comprehension in his eyes. 'I pretended that I'd had other lovers because I wanted you to believe I was over you. But I was never over you—I could never seem to stop wanting you or loving you. I invented a whole raft of fictitious lovers so that you would think I had moved on. Only I hadn't. You see, there's only ever been you, Dante. Only you.'

She watched as the implications behind her words

registered and he gave a distinctly macho smile of satisfaction.

'Oh, I *see*,' he drawled.

'Now you can kiss me,' she said.

He smoothed back the hair which was clinging to her damp cheeks and smiled. 'I've missed you, Justina.'

'You were doing a good impression of a man who was fine without me. When we came back from Tuscany it was as if you'd stopped caring completely.'

'Because I knew that I had to force your hand. I had to show you what life would be like if we split. I had to push you away in order to get you back. It was a gamble, but it was one I was prepared to take. You had to come to me because you wanted me—because you know your life would be bleak without me. Just as mine would without you.'

She lifted her hand to his face and stared into the brilliance of his eyes.

'I love you so much, Dante D'Arezzo,' she said. 'And I'm going to spend the rest of my life showing you just how much. But now, if you wouldn't mind, would you please just *kiss* me?'

EPILOGUE

JUSTINA WAS OUT in the garden when the doorbell rang. She'd been writing a song in the autumn sunshine and she glanced at Nico, sleeping peacefully in his pram, before going into the house to see who was there. Maybe Dante had forgotten his key. She hoped so. He wasn't due home for another couple of hours, but perhaps he'd managed to cut his meeting short. He was getting much better at doing that, she thought. They could take the baby for a walk to the nearby park—maybe stop off at that new coffee shop on the way home and sit at one of the tables outside.

But the figure standing on the doorstep of the Spit-alfields house was completely unexpected, and Justina stood stock-still as all kinds of conflicting emotions flooded over her. She felt resignation and slight irrita-tion—but, interestingly, the thing she felt most of all was *love* as she looked at her mother.

As usual, Elaine Perry was dressed in a style which was slightly too young for her years. Her admittedly very good figure was squeezed into a pair of jeans, and she was wearing a soft leather jacket which matched her caramel-coloured boots. From her narrow wrists clanged a symphony of narrow silver bands, and the enormous handbag she carried was one which was regularly toted by supermodels and celebrities.

'Hello, Jus,' she said.

Justina screwed up her nose. 'Well, this *is* a surprise,' she said drily. 'Where's Jacques?'

'It's Jean, actually, and he's...' The older woman gave a helpless kind of shrug. 'He's history.'

'Right.' Justina digested this. 'So, are you coming in? Or are you just passing?'

There was a moment of hesitation while Elaine Perry delved around in her bag before holding up a package. It was wrapped in shiny paper and covered with images of dancing blue teddy bears. 'I'd like to come in, if I may. I've brought a present for the baby.' She looked almost sheepish as she met Justina's eyes. 'For...Nico.'

Justina swallowed. There was so much she could have said in response to that. The old Justina might have commented that she'd thought her mother was too *young* to be a grandmother, but she had learned to think before she spoke. She had learned so much. People changed, Dante had said—and he was right. People did. She remembered what he'd said about forgiveness, too. That people couldn't be free to move on into the future if they stayed shackled to the resentments of the past. She recognised that this wasn't so much a toy that her mother was holding out towards her as an olive branch.

'You'd better come in,' she said. 'Because I know he'd just love to meet you.'

'*Would* he?'

And for the first time in her life Justina saw her mother through adult eyes. She saw the vulnerability in her face and the thick make-up which failed to cover up the deepening wrinkles. And her heart turned over.

'Of course he would, Mum,' she said softly. 'It's true he's not quite nine months old, but on some subliminal level he's bound to recognise you because you're *family*.'

Her mother was still there when Dante came home a couple of hours later, to be greeted by the rather amazing sight of two women sitting close together in the garden, the older one cradling his son.

He wondered what was going on, and then Justina looked up at him. 'Oh, you're home,' she said simply.

He smiled into her eyes and all his questions were forgotten. How could he possibly think straight when she was looking at him like that? '*Si, tesoro.* I'm home.'

Elaine Perry stayed for dinner. She told them—falteringly at first—that she was tired. Tired of being the mistress of some rich man who didn't value her. She told them how hard it was to keep up the perpetual fight to look younger than her years. It was only when she got on to the subject of leg-waxing that Justina quietly changed the subject and gave her mother another hug—though she couldn't help but worry about what the future held for someone who had only ever been reliant on the largesse of men.

It was several weeks later, when Justina and Dante were lying in bed, that she turned to him, running her fingers through his thick dark hair the way she loved to do.

'Dante?' she murmured.

'Mmm?

'You know my flat in Clerkenwell?'

'I certainly do.' He drifted a finger over her belly and felt her wriggle. 'Are you going to tell me that you're planning to sign it over to your mother?'

'You're a mind-reader!'

He smiled. 'It makes sense. She needs somewhere to live which doesn't come with the price-tag of a man—and we'll never live there as a family, will we?'

She shook her head, but his words thrilled her indescribably. *As a family.* 'No,' she said, then hesitated. 'And while we're on the subject of property...'

'You don't like this house?'

'I do. It's just...'

'Mmm?'

'It's not really where I would have chosen to live. And we didn't choose it together, did we? In fact, it was chosen when we were going through that horrible phase which I'd rather forget. I mean, if you—'

'We'll sell it,' he said instantly. 'Or rent it out. I chose this house because I wanted to be close to you, but now that we're together it doesn't matter where we live. As long as you're happy, I'm happy.'

'Oh, Dante,' she whispered. 'I love you so much.'

'I know you do. And the best thing of all is that I feel exactly the same way about you.' His smile was tender as he pulled her closer. 'So tell me—are you looking forward to our wedding?'

Was she? She couldn't wait! They were flying out to Tuscany to be married at the *palazzo*, and Dante had taken off a whole month for their honeymoon.

She suspected that he wanted to move out to Italy permanently, and she was going to tell him that she was perfectly amenable to the idea. She'd even restarted her Italian lessons in preparation, and this time around she was taking them much more seriously. And the great thing about her job was that you could do it just about anywhere.

In fact she was in the middle of writing a song which she hadn't yet shown him, but she thought it might be the best thing she'd ever done. It was called *Forever*— and it was a powerful tribute to the man she would always love.

Forever.

* * * * *

A sneaky peek at next month...

MODERN™

INTERNATIONAL AFFAIRS, SEDUCTION & PASSION GUARANTEED

My wish list for next month's titles...

In stores from 15th March 2013:

❏ Master of her Virtue – Miranda Lee

❏ A Taste of the Forbidden – Carole Mortimer

❏ The Merciless Travis Wilde – Sandra Marton

❏ Heir to a Desert Legacy – Maisey Yates

In stores from 5th April 2013:

❏ The Cost of her Innocence – Jacqueline Baird

❏ Count Valieri's Prisoner – Sara Craven

❏ A Game with One Winner – Lynn Raye Harris

❏ The Sinful Art of Revenge – Maya Blake

❏ Marriage in Name Only? – Anne Oliver

Available at WHSmith, Tesco, Asda, Eason, Amazon and Apple

Just can't wait?

Visit us Online

You can buy our books online a month before they hit the shops! **www.millsandboon.co.uk**

0313/01

Special Offers

Every month we put together collections and longer reads written by your favourite authors.

Here are some of next month's highlights—and don't miss our fabulous discount online!

On sale 5th April

On sale 15th March

On sale 5th April

Find out more at
www.millsandboon.co.uk/specialreleases

Visit us Online

0413/ST/MB410

MILLS & BOON® *Book Club*

Save over £40

Join the Mills & Boon Book Club

Subscribe to **Modern**™ today for 3, 6 or 12 months and you could **save over £40!**

We'll also treat you to these fabulous extras:

- 🌹 **FREE L'Occitane gift set worth £10**
- 🌹 **FREE home delivery**
- 🌹 **Books up to 2 months ahead of the shops**
- 🌹 **Bonus books, exclusive offers... and much more!**

Subscribe now at
www.millsandboon.co.uk/subscribeme

Visit us Online

Save over £40 – find out more at
www.millsandboon.co.uk/subscrlbome

SUBS/OFFER/P

The World of Mills & Boon®

There's a Mills & Boon® series that's perfect for you. We publish ten series and, with new titles every month, you never have to wait long for your favourite to come along.

Scorching hot, sexy reads
4 new stories every month

By Request
Relive the romance with the best of the best
9 new stories every month

Cherish™
Romance to melt the heart every time
12 new stories every month

Desire™
Passionate and dramatic love stories
8 new stories every month

Visit us Online
Try something new with our Book Club offer
www.millsandboon.co.uk/freebookoffer

M&B/WORLD2

What will you treat yourself to next?

Ignite your imagination,
step into the past...
6 new stories every month

INTRIGUE...

Breathtaking romantic suspense
Up to 8 new stories every month

 Medical Romance

Captivating medical drama –
with heart
6 new stories every month

MODERN™

International affairs,
seduction & passion guaranteed
9 new stories every month

nocturne™

Deliciously wicked
paranormal romance
Up to 4 new stories every month

RIVA™

Live life to the full –
give in to temptation
3 new stories every month available
exclusively via our Book Club

You can also buy Mills & Boon eBooks at
www.millsandboon.co.uk

 Visit us Online

M&B/WORLD2

Mills & Boon® Online

Discover more romance at
www.millsandboon.co.uk

 FREE online reads

 Books up to one
month before shops

 Browse our books
before you buy

...and much more!

For exclusive competitions and instant updates:

 Like us on **facebook.com/romancehq**

 Follow us on **twitter.com/millsandboonuk**

 Join us on **community.millsandboon.co.uk**

 Visit us Online   Sign up for our FREE eNewsletter at
www.millsandboon.co.uk

WEB/M&B/RTL4